MAY   2014

Ten Turtles on Tuesday

Ten Turtles on Tuesday

A Story for Children
About Obsessive-Compulsive Disorder

by Ellen Flanagan Burns
illustrated by Sue Cornelison

MAGINATION PRESS · WASHINGTON, DC
American Psychological Association

For my brother, Ed. —EFB

Published by
MAGINATION PRESS
An Educational Publishing Foundation Book
American Psychological Association
750 First Street, NE
Washington, DC 20002

For more information about our books, including a complete catalog, please write to us, call 1-800-374-2721, or visit our website at www.apa.org/pubs/magination.

Printed by Phoenix Color Corporation, Hagerstown, MD
Book designed by Susan K. White

Library of Congress Cataloging-in-Publication Data
Burns, Ellen Flanagan.
Ten turtles on Tuesday : a story for children about obsessive-compulsive disorder / by Ellen Flanagan Burns ; illustrated by Sue Cornelison.
pages cm
"American Psychological Association."
"An Educational Publishing Foundation Book."
Summary: Eleven-year-old Sarah is confused, embarrassed, and frustrated by her need to count things but finally talks with her mother and a therapist, who diagnoses Obsessive-Compulsive Disorder and gives Sarah techniques for coping with her symptoms. Includes note to readers.
ISBN 978-1-4338-1643-7 (hardcover) — ISBN 1-4338-1643-1 (hardcover) — ISBN 978-1-4338-1644-4 (pbk.) — ISBN 1-4338-1644-X (pbk.) [1. Obsessive-compulsive disorder—Fiction. 2. Emotional problems—Fiction. 3. Family life—Fiction.] I. Cornelison, Sue, illustrator. II. Title.
PZ7.B9366Ten 2013   [Fic]—dc23
2013020712

Manufactured in the United States of America
First printing September 2013
10 9 8 7 6 5 4 3 2 1

Contents

Dear Reader 6

Chapter 1: Sarah 9

Chapter 2: WildWorld 13

Chapter 3: Counting 19

Chapter 4: Fidgety Fish....................... 23

Chapter 5: What If.............................. 27

Chapter 6: The King............................. 31

Chapter 7: What's OCD?..................... 37

Chapter 8: The Good Detective 41

Chapter 9: The OCD Game.................. 47

Chapter 10: Pretzels or Potato Chips 53

Chapter 11: Wearing out Its Welcome............... 57

Chapter 12: Resisting the Urge 63

Chapter 13: In the Driver's Seat 67

Note to Readers................................... 72

About the Author and Illustrator 80

Dear Reader

Do you ever feel like you have to do something over and over? Maybe you count. Maybe you wash your hands, or check to make sure something is right. Maybe you clean, or perform certain actions with your body, or ask for reassurances. Maybe you do a combination of these things, or something completely different.

In *Ten Turtles on Tuesday*, you'll meet a girl named Sarah. Sarah feels like she has to count over and over or something bad might happen, like her mom might die. That's a heavy burden to carry! She counts things in order to feel better, but it never works for very long, and it only ends up making her feel worse.

Sarah has obsessive-compulsive disorder, or OCD for short. Lots of people have OCD. If you're one of them, you can do something about it.

Obsessions are upsetting thoughts that come back again and again. They come from our fears and make us feel an exaggerated sense of danger. Sarah worries that something bad might happen to her mom. Obsessions are usually about something bad happening to ourselves or someone we love.

Compulsions are something we do over and over to feel protected, like how Sarah opens and closes her closet door a certain number of times. Compulsions are actually a clever way to feel better at first, until we do them too much. The urge to do them is very strong. The truth is, most people repeat certain behaviors from time to time, but when it interferes with your life and upsets you, it's time to do something about it.

By giving in to your urges, you're giving your obsessions and compulsions more credit than they deserve. That makes them stronger. If you think of your obsession as a weed in your garden, then your compulsion is the water that feeds it, making it grow. You can choose to give in to an urge, or wait until it goes away.

It will take courage for you to wait until it goes away. At first, you'll feel anxiety, maybe a whole lot of anxiety. Your heart might pound. You might shake. You might get sweaty. You might get angry and irritable. But if you just feel the feelings without doing anything about them, they will go away all by themselves—just like waves in the ocean rising and crashing on the beach. Before you know it, it will get easier to resist your urges.

Some people wonder if OCD is the same as worrying. It's not. Worries—such as "What if I'm not good enough to make the team?" or "What if I don't have anyone to sit with at lunch?"—come and go. With OCD, the same upsetting thoughts come back over and over.

You might be wondering how I know about this. When I was a young girl I struggled with OCD. I remember one day making the decision to stop giving in to my urges. I said, "Enough is enough!" and I got out of the OCD game. Every now and then the urges came back. It was hard, but I knew that if I ignored them, they would go away again. Sure enough, they did!

Are you ready to be free from OCD? You can do it. I'm rooting for you.

Your friend,
Ellen

CHAPTER ONE

Sarah

Dear Diary,

We're getting close to WildWorld. We just passed the old gas station on the right and the little store with the red and green roof. I counted the whole way—5 of us, 5 taps on my leg, 2 kids playing in a sprinkler, 6 cars on the side of the road. Seems like I count more than ever. I can't help it. Nobody else in the car counts stuff— I can tell. They sing songs and think about whatever they want. When Mom taps the steering wheel it's for fun, to the beat of the song, not because she has to. I wish I could be like that, so carefree.

Sometimes I ask Mom if she notices how many houses are on the block, or how many people are on the sidewalk, but she never does. So I count secretly to myself...because I know it's Weird.

"Let's go, Sarah!" Mom called again, a little louder this time. We were running late because of me, as usual. "I'll be there in a minute!" I called back. I didn't want to keep her waiting, but I had to be sure my closet door was shut *just right*. So I opened it again and closed it, opened it again and closed it again.

My cat, Lucky, sat at my window watching blue jays gather around the birdfeeder. Crickets chirped from the grass. Yellow tulips bloomed in the garden. It was a warm spring day with no school, and we were headed to an amusement park, WildWorld, with my best friend Kaelyn, my little brother Tommy, and his friend.

"Just two more times," I whispered to myself as I opened the closet door again, then closed it again, opened it again, and closed it again.

Kaelyn and I met seven years ago when her family moved all the way from Chicago into the house across the street. We were only five, but it feels like yesterday: sitting on the driveway with my dad, watching the movers unload their things—a kitchen table, sofa, suitcases, bikes—a steady stream that seemed to go on and on forever. I hoped a new friend was moving in, a girl my age. Then Kaelyn and her mom walked over with a brown and white puppy.

"WOOF!" the puppy barked, his little tail wagging back and forth quickly as if waving hello.

"This is Sporty," Kaelyn said. "He won't hurt

you." Sporty licked my cheek. I liked my new friends right away.

"Sarah!" Mom called again. She was losing patience.

Then my little brother Tommy called, "COME ON, SARAH!!" He ran up the stairs and banged on my bedroom door. They were in a hurry to get to the park. I was too. The pressure was building, like a balloon about to pop. And it was my fault. But it was worse when they interrupted me, because then I had to start over.

"Almost ready!" I called, as I opened the closet door again and closed it, then opened it again.

I heard my mom calling Kaelyn's mom. "I'm sorry, we're running late. We shouldn't be too much longer." I felt ashamed for making them wait. *Why was I doing this?* And why was it happening more and more?

"Coming!" I yelled, closing the door for the last time. It finally felt right. I was free! What a relief. I rushed to put on my sneakers and grabbed my bag. Out of the corner of my eye I saw Mom with her arms crossed. She looked mad. I didn't like to upset her. One time I heard about a man that was so mad he had a heart attack and died right on the spot. I didn't want that to happen to Mom.

"Sorry, Mom, I was cleaning my room." I knew it was a lie, but if I told her what I was really doing, she'd be even madder. Wouldn't she?

CHAPTER TWO
WildWorld

Dear Diary,

I'm so embarrassed. Today at WildWorld I was so worried about Mom that I had to run out of the line to check on her. Kaelyn probably thought I was being super weird.

I want to tell her why I did it, but it probably wouldn't make any sense... would it? I don't know why I get so worried about stuff. I wish I could have just enjoyed the rides and the ice cream like everybody else.

"Whoa! Check out the new roller coaster!" Kaelyn pointed to it as we drove into the parking lot of WildWorld. The "Python" coaster rose up to the sky and wound its way around the park like a snake circling its prey.

"Sweet!" Tommy yelled. We all high-fived.

"Stick together and meet me back here for lunch by 12:30!" Mom called after us. She had packed a cooler full of turkey and Swiss cheese sandwiches on whole wheat bread, pickles, chips, and pink lemonade. She placed her bags on a picnic table and settled in to her mystery novel. Reading was one of her favorite things to do.

Kaelyn and I roamed the park, taking it all in. We could smell buttery popcorn in the air. There were so many things to do: the waterslide to the right, bumper cars to the left, the Zipper and Scrambler rides after that, and a pirate ship ride farther along.

First we rode the Himalaya. The cars sped around fast in a circle, first forward, then backward, while the speakers blared Michael Jackson's "Don't Stop 'til You Get Enough."

Next to the ride was a small shack with an ice cream swirl for a roof. It was an old-fashioned ice cream stand that also sold pink and blue cotton candy and snow cones.

Six people in line getting cones, and three people working behind the counter equals nine. Then three more people get in line, which equals twelve all together.

We rode the Spider, a menacing-looking ride that looked just like a real spider, with eight legs moving in a circle, each leg holding a spinning cart.

We thought about going on the waterslide. *Eight kids on a waterslide, and three waterslides all together equals eleven. I tapped my leg eleven times. Eleven plus eleven equals twenty-two.*

But we hopped in line for the Python roller coaster instead. As we waited in line, I noticed a dark cloud moving in, promising to bring rain later in the day. I thought about Mom and wondered if she was okay. She was quiet in the car this morning; maybe she didn't feel good. *Two taps on my leg.* "What if mom's sick?" I thought. I had a funny feeling she was. *Eighteen people in front of us in line and seven people behind us. Eighteen plus seven equals twenty-five, plus twenty-five taps on my leg equals fifty.* Counting usually helped me feel better, but it wasn't working quickly enough.

The line moved a little closer. What if a storm came through, and everyone had to run for safety? I've heard about things like that happening. I imagined Mom needing help. What if she really did? I had to fix this before I got on the ride or something bad would happen. I just knew it. My heart beat fast in my chest. *Five carts on the roller coaster—one, two, three, four, five—plus five taps on my leg equals ten.* It still wasn't working. I had to go see Mom; it was the only thing that would help me feel better.

"Hold our spot. I'll be right back!" I shouted over my shoulder to Kaelyn.

"Sarah, wait!" Kaelyn called after me.

But I didn't listen. There was no time to explain and it probably wouldn't make any sense anyway. I ran as fast as I could, weaving in and out of the crowd until I finally reached Mom back at the picnic table. "Is everything okay?" I asked. I was out of breath and a little shaky.

Mom looked up from her book, startled. "Sarah?"

"Are you okay?" I asked again.

"Of course. Why? Is everything okay with you kids?"

"Yes, I mean…oh, never mind. I just had a funny feeling something was wrong." Mom looked confused. I felt relieved, but a little silly at the same time. I ran back to meet Kaelyn, and made it there just in time for our turn—or so I thought.

"No cutting in line," the ride operator told me.

"But…" I protested.

"No cutting in line," he reiterated.

It was no use. We went to the back of the line to wait all over again. Now I *really* felt embarrassed.

"What happened? Where did you go?" Kaelyn asked.

"I had to go see my mom."

"Why?"

"I was afraid there was something wrong, like maybe she didn't feel good or something."

"Next time I'll go with you. We should stick together, like your mom said."

I agreed. "Sorry."

CHAPTER THREE
Counting

Dear Diary,

I'm so tired of counting everything I could scream! Closing my closet door 10 times, eating a bowl of cereal in 12 bites, taking 8 steps from the stairs to the door. Even in school—counting the buses as they pull up, the brushes in Miss Mack's art class, or the number of desks. Bedtime is even worse—touching my toothbrush over and over, and other stuff too.

P.S. Miss Mack has 36 brushes! Counting helps me feel better for a little while, but then I do it more and more and it drives me crazy! I think if I do it just one more time, I'll never have to do it again—but then I do.

P.P.S. I missed the bus again because of it. Mom gets mad when she has to drive me to school. I wish I could stop. I wish, I wish!!

What if I tell Mom and Dad about it? I wonder what they'd say. It probably wouldn't make any sense to them. They'd say, "Just stop!" But I can't. I don't know why. What's wrong with me? Am I crazy?

I lay in bed listening to the rain on the roof. It was coming down heavy, in buckets. "It's a perfect day to work on your project," Mom said over breakfast. "The forecast says it's not letting up." I agreed. I was excited about my collection of Native American artifacts made by the Cherokees and Navajos a long time ago. I was going to write a description for each piece.

I gathered my collection of artifacts and arranged them on my bedroom floor, admiring each one. They were mostly arrowheads that I found when I was digging in Dad's garden and when I was walking through the woods near my house. I also had a couple of tools, a few pieces of jewelry that belonged to Mom, a basket and some pottery. Dad and I bought some of it online.

I counted each arrowhead and touched its slippery surface. I was glad there were eight of them all together, because that's an even number. When I count stuff, it always has to add up to an even number because odd numbers don't feel right—it's like they're bad luck or something. So if I only had three arrowheads—an odd number—I would have to leave one out or keep looking for one more to reach an even number. Or sometimes I can just tap my leg the same number of times to feel better. Like three arrowheads and three taps on my leg equals six, an even number.

I counted the arrowheads over and over as I touched each one. I kept thinking that I had to wait for it to feel right before I could move on and work on my project, or something bad would happen to the project. "One, two, three, four..." I felt stuck.

Lucky pushed his head through the crack of my bedroom door and walked in. I was happy to see him, glad for the interruption. "This is a bad day for counting," I told him. I explained what happened earlier. "I took seven steps to the door by accident—an odd number—and I had to go back and do it right. Tommy saw what I was doing and thought it would be fun to try and block me. I got so mad at him that I pushed him and called him mean names."

Lucky rubbed his head in my hand. I went on, "And I took sixty-one seconds to make a sandwich—an odd number—so I had to start over! I ended up using a whole loaf of bread before I got it right. Mom wondered where all the bread went. From now on I won't look at the clock when I make a sandwich, Lucky. And it took forever to fill your water bowl! I kept filling it and dumping it until it finally felt right."

Lucky purred and curled up for a nap next to me. I noticed I didn't need to count the arrowheads anymore. I was starting to feel better. I thanked him for the help and got to work on my project. I hoped I could finish it before I had to count again.

CHAPTER FOUR

Fidgety Fish

Dear Diary,

I want to stop counting, but if I do,
I worry that something bad might happen.
So I keep doing it to be on the safe side.
It's like there's an annoying mosquito
buzzing around my ear saying,
"You better count or you'll be sorry."
It makes me nervous. When I count,
it helps me feel better—for a little while.
The mosquito flies away, but it always
comes back!!

"The last seed is planted!" Dad called to Tommy and me. He rented a small plot of land from the farmer down the street. Every spring, we planted a vegetable garden. Then, when summer arrived, we picked the vegetables: shiny green bell peppers, giant red tomatoes, and sweet corn.

Once a week, Tommy and I helped him water the plants and pull the weeds. It sounds easy, but it's not. It's hard work. We had to walk down to the stream, fill up buckets with water, and carry them back to water the plants.

Today we were digging in the garden to loosen the soil, plant the seeds, and water them for the first time.

"Whoa! Dad, look, a baby fish!" Tommy shouted, pointing to a tiny fish swimming around his bucket. "I think he wants to go back to the stream."

We walked back to the stream together to let it go. "This reminds me of the story of the fidgety fish," Dad said. "Would you like to hear it?"

We nodded. It was a good time to take a break—our arms were getting tired from carrying the buckets of water. We turned our buckets upside down and sat on them.

"Once upon a time, there was a happy little fish that swam fast around his big fish tank. He loved to feel the cool, rippling water against his face as he darted all around. His favorite game was to hide within the tall grass or behind the coral and jump out at his friends when they swam by. One day he noticed an opening at the top of the tank. 'Uh oh. If the tank tips over, I'll fall out and die,' he thought. So, from then on, he stayed still to keep the tank steady. He watched the others swimming around and having fun, but he wouldn't join them. He felt scared and mad."

"That doesn't make sense!" Tommy said. "Fish can't tip over their tanks. Right, Dad?!"

"No, it's not likely."

"But what if he did? It's better to be safe than sorry," I said, defending the fish. "Right, Dad?"

"Only when it makes sense," Dad said.

"That's true. His fears *were* a little exaggerated," I admitted. "After a while the fish probably realized it was safe to swim."

Tommy finished the story. "So the little fish started swimming around again and having fun."

"I like that ending," Dad said.

"Staying still helped him feel safe for a little while, but it didn't really do any good and it only made him fidgety," I said.

"It wasn't a good solution," Dad agreed.

Sort of like me and counting, I thought to myself. At first it helped me feel better, but then I ended up feeling like the fidgety fish.

CHAPTER FIVE

What If...

Dear Diary,

I wish I could be more like Kaelyn. She's not afraid something bad might happen, like I am. She must feel as light as a feather. Me, I wear my fears like a big heavy coat. They come out of nowhere, when I least expect it, like little pieces of popcorn popping up. Like what if a tree falls on our house?...POP!... or what if Dad gets hurt at work?... POP, POP!...or, worst of all, what if Mom gets sick? What if she dies? I wish I didn't think about it so much.

On the way to school I sit with Kaelyn—when I don't miss the bus. Sometimes we have so much fun I forget to count.

On Monday morning, Kaelyn and I reminisced about the trip to WildWorld last week. She liked getting soaked on the waterslide, and how the pink cotton candy melted on her tongue. I liked the spooky funhouse with its creepy noises and scary surprises around every corner.

We both had soft serve ice cream cones—mine was vanilla with chocolate sprinkles and Kaelyn's was an orange and vanilla twist. We tried to remember the name of the girl who gave us the cones. She was ahead of us in school. "It begins with a K...Kim!" Kaelyn said.

"That's it! It was nice of the manager to let her give us extra ice cream."

Our favorite ride was the Python roller coaster. "When we hit that drop, I felt like I was going to barf!" Kaelyn said.

"Remember the Zipper? When your water flew out of your hands?" I asked.

"We both yelled, 'Oh no!' at the same time," Kaelyn laughed. Then her voice got quieter and she said, "Hey, when you left the line for the Python...I was so worried. I thought you were hurt or there was an emergency. Why'd you do that? It was kind of weird."

My cheeks felt hot. I knew what I was about

to say wouldn't make any sense. "I couldn't stop thinking about my mom. I thought she might be sick or something."

"Why would you think that? She would've told you if she was sick, wouldn't she?"

"I guess so." Kaelyn had a good point. But I wanted to explain. "Remember when Jill's mom died last year, and she had to miss the last part of the semester?"

Kaelyn nodded.

"Sometimes I'm afraid that will happen to my mom. Aren't you?"

"When it first happened I was, but honestly, I don't really think about it anymore."

I couldn't believe she didn't think about it. "Why not?"

"Well, why would I? I mean, my mom's healthy, and that sort of thing doesn't usually happen. Besides, thinking about it all the time isn't going to help anything. Is it?"

"No, I guess not," I said. I knew that was true. "But what if it *did* happen?"

"Well, it would be awful. But I figure my family would be there for me and I'd be there for them. And I could count on you too, right?"

I nodded.

"So eventually I'd be okay, I guess. Like Jill."

Our bus pulled into school.

"It's the same for you," she added.

CHAPTER SIX
The King

Dear Diary,

I was so worried about telling Mom and Dad about how I count...
I thought they would think I was crazy, or that there was something wrong with me. It turns out I can talk to them after all. It feels good to talk to them and know that they are going to be there to help me.

They said I don't have to count because no matter what I'll be okay. But what if I stop counting and something bad happens? That scares me.

"Knock, knock," Mom came in to my room to say goodnight.

"I have a story," I told her.

"Let's hear it," Mom said, and sat down next to my bed. We liked making up our own stories.

"Once there was a king who was afraid of his kingdom falling apart. So he made up tons of rules to protect it, like everyone had to act like monkeys on Monday, collect ten turtles on Tuesday, walk backwards on Wednesday, never step on thorns on Thursday, and find five fireflies on Friday."

"Those are strange rules," Mom said.

"I know. But the king said they were really important, so even though they seemed silly, the people followed them anyway just to be on the safe side."

"What a pain."

"I know; it was. The king was so busy looking for turtles and making up new rules that he never had any fun. It was a big waste of time," I explained.

"Oh...what if he talked to the queen about his

Royal Decree

* Act like monkeys on Monday

* Collect ten turtles on Tuesday

* Walk backwards on Wednesday

* Never step on thorns on Thursday

32

fears? If his kingdom ever fell apart, I'm sure she would help him rebuild it."

"Maybe. But he was afraid she wouldn't understand."

"Well, we all need help sometimes." Mom added, gently, "You know, when something's bothering you, Sarah, you can talk to your dad and me."

I wanted to tell her about my problems, but I was nervous. Would she think I was silly? Would she think I was weird?

"Mom, sometimes I count things...a lot..." Mom put her arms around me. "...And I can't stop, no matter how hard I try."

"I've done things like that too," Mom said. "But not as much. Sometimes I check once or twice to make sure the stove and iron are turned off before I go to bed, even when I know they are. That's because I think about being safe. What do *you* think about?" she asked.

I knew the answer. "That something really bad will happen." I started to cry. I was tired of having these thoughts and tired of counting. "I'm even afraid you'll die."

"When did this start?" Mom wondered.

"Remember when Jill's mom died?"

Mom nodded. She thought Jill was a sweet girl.

"Ever since then. Sometimes in school I don't even pay attention, and when the intercom comes on I'm afraid they're going to call me into the office and tell me something bad happened. Maybe the house burned down or you were in an accident or something." I cried some more.

"That would be very unlikely," Mom said gently. Then she said, "Remember the squirrel that fell from the tree branch into the snow?"

"Yeah, luckily the snow was there to protect him, like a safety net," I said.

"And off he ran, up the tree again. Life's like that—full of ups and downs, but you'll be okay," Mom assured me.

"But what if something bad happens?" I asked. "Like what if Dad loses his job or you get in an accident?"

"Well, that's not likely to happen, but even if it did, we would work it out. We would be okay."

"But what if you died?"

"I don't plan on dying anytime soon. But even if I did, I would want you to enjoy your life. You still have lots of things to do."

Just then, Dad poked his head in the door. He must have heard our conversation from the hallway. "Yeah, like being president of the United States."

I giggled.

"Dad! You know I don't want to be the president! I want to be a veterinarian!"

Sometimes we played "What will you be when you grow up?" I used to want to be a baker, then an astronaut. Now, I dreamed of being a veterinarian.

"But if Mom died, I wouldn't do anything. I'd curl up in a ball forever."

"Then who would help the sick animals?" Dad asked.

Mom chimed in, "You would have to put a sign on your office door: 'I can't take care of your pets today—or any day!—since I never went to vet school. Sorry.'"

I giggled some more.

"And what about Dad and Tommy?" Mom added.

"Okay, okay, I get the picture!" I threw my hands up. We laughed together and I wiped away my tears. I wouldn't do that to all those poor animals! Or my family. It was true: I had things to do, no matter what. So maybe I *would* be okay, no matter what.

"And all of your dreams and interests and the important people in your life are like one big safety net," Mom said.

CHAPTER SEVEN

What's OCD?

Dear Diary,

Today I met with a therapist named Dr. Goode. Mom and Dad say she helps people and she can help me too. I thought she would think I was dumb or weird for counting. But it turns out she was pretty easy to talk to after all. She felt like a new friend.

She said counting like I do helps me feel protected. It's called OCD. Other people wash their hands a lot, or check on things over and over, and other stuff too.

But will she **really** be able to help me stop counting???

Mom and Dad came along with me to meet Dr. Goode. She had a cool office with lots of books, a desk, two comfy brown chairs, and three big, squishy beanbag chairs on the floor. She collects antique lamps. So far she has four, all of them different shapes and sizes. They're pretty, like little pieces of art. My favorite one is made out of light green glass and filled with seashells. It has purple irises painted on the lampshade.

Dr. Goode listened to us, and asked some questions too. She understood what I was going through. When I finished telling her about the counting, she said, "You're not dumb or weird, Sarah. You're a smart girl. You have obsessive-compulsive disorder, or OCD for short."

"What's OCD?" I asked.

"OCD is when your mind gets stuck on a thought, making you feel anxious, as if you're in danger."

"Like worrying about stuff?"

"No, worries come and go. What you're describing is an obsession. An obsession is an upsetting thought that stays with you."

"Like thinking something bad might happen or my mom might die."

"Yes. So you've come up with this clever way to feel better."

"By counting!"

"Yes, counting helps you feel protected, so that's why you do it. When we do something over and over again, like counting, it's called a compulsion," she explained. "*Counting* is a common way to feel protected, but some people *clean*, or *arrange* things in a certain way, or *wash their hands*. Other people feel protected when they *check* something over and over, or do certain *body movements* like tapping or humming, or *actions* like turning a light on and off. And some people *save* so much stuff that it gets in the way. Compulsions take up a lot of time."

"So I'm not the only one with OCD," I said.

"No, I've helped many others."

I felt relieved.

"The truth is, most people repeat certain behaviors from time to time. But when it interferes with your life and upsets you, then it's not the best solution," Dr. Goode explained. "We'll find better solutions together."

CHAPTER EIGHT

The Good Detective

Dear Diary,

I'm getting good at telling the difference between my obsessions and my regular thoughts. My obsessions make me feel nervous, like there's danger all around, when there really isn't. They come from my fears. Fears like, "What if Mom dies or what if she gets sick?" I'm learning to let them go, like little balloons in the air, floating away on their own.

Dr. Goode says that a thought is just a thought. My thoughts don't have to control me!

"Counting only protects me for a little while, and then I have to do it again," I told Dr. Goode at our next visit.

"That's a big burden to carry," Mom said. She gave me a hug.

I agreed. "I'm tired of it."

"I can help you with this," Dr. Goode assured me.

"How?"

"The first step is discovering you're not in danger after all. Let's see...what would you say if I told you that I stayed awake all night just in case a monster *might be* in my closet?" Dr. Goode asked me.

"I would tell you to look in the closet and see, like a detective. It might be scary, but at least you'd know for sure."

"That's great advice! It's good to look and see if our ideas make sense. When I look in the closet, I'll see there's no monster and then I'll feel better," Dr. Goode said.

I nodded.

"So, be a good detective—look and see if counting protects you from danger," Dr. Goode suggested.

"How?"

"Well, first, you could think about how much sense it makes," she said.

"It doesn't make any sense, I know, but what if..." I hesitated. "What if counting really *does* help for some weird reason?"

"Well, a good detective also tests out her ideas to

see if they're correct."

"You mean I could see what happens when I *don't* count?"

"Yes."

"I'd probably see that nothing bad happens—just like looking in the closet and seeing that there's no monster."

"Yes, you would discover that everything's okay after all..."

"...that there's no danger, whether I count or not," I said. "So I guess there would be no need for protection. Counting would seem sort of lame after that—pretty useless."

"And what would that tell you about your obsessions?" Dr. Goode asked.

"That they're not very trustworthy," I answered. I had never thought of it that way.

"Excellent detective work!" Dr. Goode said.

My obsessions were different from my regular thoughts, I realized. "But why would my obsessions lie to me like that?" I wondered.

"Somewhere along the line, your fears became exaggerated," Dr. Goode explained.

"So I end up feeling like there's an emergency when there isn't," I said.

"Yes. Counting helps you get through the emergency."

"Until the next one."

Dr. Goode nodded. "When that happens—when

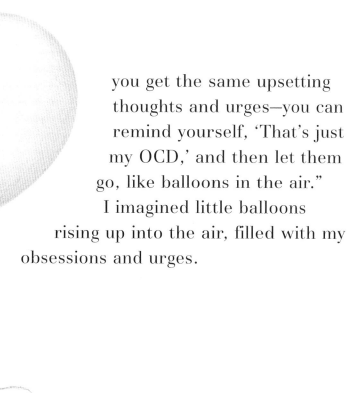

you get the same upsetting
thoughts and urges—you can
remind yourself, 'That's just
my OCD,' and then let them
go, like balloons in the air."
I imagined little balloons
rising up into the air, filled with my
obsessions and urges.

CHAPTER NINE

The OCD Game

Dear Diary,

Today I imagined my OCD thoughts were weeds in my garden, and counting was the water that was feeding them, making them grow. It's up to me whether I water them or not! I don't want to anymore. It'll be hard to stop counting, but maybe I can do it. I know I'll feel really nervous and grumpy, but it can't last forever. I can remind myself, "That's just my OCD talking!" or I can say, "I'm not playing the OCD game!" That will help me feel stronger.

Will it really get easier the more I do it, like Dr. Goode says??

"I feel like I'm in a game with OCD and I'm losing," I told Dr. Goode the next time I saw her. "I keep counting because it's quicker and easier, but the more I do it, the more my urges come back."

Dr. Goode nodded. "OCD *is* like a game in a way. It's sort of like a game of volleyball that needs two players, obsessions *and* compulsions. Your obsessions and compulsions work together, keeping the ball in the air. First you have a thought, then you count, then you have a thought again, and so on, back and forth. If you wanted to get out of the game, what could you do?"

"I could stop counting, I guess." It made sense. "Just like if I wanted to stop playing volleyball, I would stop hitting the ball back to my opponent."

Dr. Goode said, "Yes, very good!"

"But it's too hard. Resisting my urges makes me feel nervous and grumpy," I told her.

Dr. Goode nodded. "Feelings come and go, sort of like waves in an ocean."

I imagined a big wave rising up and crashing on the beach.

"That nervous feeling won't last forever," Dr. Goode explained. "It will rise up like a wave, but then it will go away all by itself if you give it a chance."

Dr. Goode was probably right. I

should just wait until the urge goes away instead of giving in to it. But I wondered if she knew how strong my urges were. "My urges feel like the Big Bad Wolf threatening to blow my house down unless I give in to them."

Dr. Goode nodded. "I understand. It will take courage, but you can do it. And it will get easier the more you do it. Sometimes it helps if someone sits with you," she added.

I thought of Mom and Dad. I knew they would sit with me if I needed them.

"In the meantime, let's talk about ways to build up your house nice and strong. Getting a good night's sleep is important. So is eating good food, like fruits and vegetables, instead of too much candy."

"I noticed when I took a yoga class with mom last week and we breathed really deep and stretched for a whole hour, we both felt good afterward. I didn't obsess or count much that day."

"Great idea!"

"We're doing more yoga, starting Friday!" I said.

Dr. Goode explained that sometimes taking medicine for OCD helps too.

"I notice I don't count much when I'm having fun or I'm interested in something," I told her.
"It pushes the OCD away for a while."

"Good observation! We can't control our thoughts, but we can shift our attention. It's like lowering the volume on TV. You hold the remote and you can turn down the volume on your obsession until it goes away," Dr. Goode explained. "When your imagination runs wild with ideas like, 'What if Mom's sick?' or 'What if Dad's hurt?' try lowering the volume on your obsession by shifting your attention to something fun or interesting instead."

"Like…'What if I make a new friend in school this year?' Or 'What if I learn to sew? I bet I could make some cool clothes.' I like that better."

"You got it! It might take some practice but you'll get the hang of it," Dr. Goode said. "Imagine you're going to the store with your mom. You walk to the car and sitting in the driver's seat is the Big Bad Wolf. Would you let him drive?"

"No way!" I said. "I'd run away as fast as I could."

"When you give in to your urges, it's as if you're letting them drive, like they're in control."

"But it's my life. I'm the driver!" I told her. I felt mad when I thought of it that way.

I was starting to see that resisting the urge was the best thing to do. If I could resist the urge and wait until it went away, I could get out of the OCD game.

CHAPTER TEN

Pretzels or Potato Chips

Dear Diary,

OCD used to be so confusing,
kind of like a mystery. I used to
think I didn't have any say over it,
that I just had to deal with it.
But now I know I do. It reminds
me of the Wizard of Oz, when
Dorothy realizes there's a man
behind the curtain. The Wizard
doesn't seem so strong and powerful
after that. Dr. Goode is helping me
pull back the curtain on OCD. There's
hope after all, Diary. Stay tuned...

"Once there was a boy who ate pretzels all the time, day and night. Pretzels, pretzels, pretzels!" Mom was sitting at the side of my bed, listening to my bedtime story. "He went to the pretzel machine, put in his money, pushed the button, and got pretzels. It was predictable and easy, and they were good. Eventually, the boy grew tired of pretzels and wanted something else. There was a potato chip machine nearby, but he was afraid to use it. 'What if it doesn't work? What if it costs too much? What if the chips are stale?' he wondered. So even though he didn't want them anymore, he kept buying pretzels to be on the safe side. He would go to the pretzel machine and pray that by some miracle, potato chips would come out. Then one day he put in his money, and pushed the button, and guess what happened?"

"Potato chips finally came out?" Mom asked hopefully.

"No, he got more pretzels!" We laughed.

"How frustrating!" Mom exclaimed.

"I know. Then, one day, he noticed that other people seemed pretty happy with their potato chips. The chips didn't look stale at all, and the machine seemed to work just fine. He even checked out the price and they were cheaper than the pretzels! So even though he was nervous, he gathered up all of his courage and walked to the potato chip machine. He put in his money, pushed the button, and out fell potato chips. 'Awesome,' he thought."

"He finally did something different!" Mom said.

"And he finally got what he wanted," I added.

"I guess if you really want potato chips, you should stop going to the pretzel machine."

I agreed. "And Dr. Goode says if I really want my urges to go away, then I should stop giving in to them. We figured out that it's probably safe for me to stop counting."

Mom asked, "Are you ready?"

"I don't know." I shrugged. "It'll be hard to resist the urges, but if I wait long enough, I'll be okay."

"Kind of like jumping into a cold pool." Mom said. "If you wait long enough you get used to it and it feels fine."

"Yeah. Exactly. So, I'm off to the potato chip machine!" I joked. I went to the bathroom to brush my teeth...*touched the toothbrush four times... looked at my reflection in the bathroom mirror once, twice, and two more times equals four... closed my closet door and opened it...closed it again and opened it again. I took six steps across my room and hopped into bed.*

Mom pulled up the blanket and kissed me goodnight.

CHAPTER ELEVEN
Wearing out Its Welcome

Dear Diary,

Counting helped me feel safe, but I don't think I need it so much anymore. I'm ready to stop counting all the time!! I know I'll feel nervous at first, but I think I can do it. I think I can handle my fears. I'm starting on Monday—hey, that's tomorrow! All week long, I'm not opening and closing my closet door! Dr. Goode said to start slow and add more things later, when I'm ready. I can't wait! I'm going to show OCD who's boss!

P.S. Enough is enough!!
P.P.S. Yoga is the best! It helps me feel good. And it's fun taking classes with Mom.

"….one, two, three, four," I counted
everything on my dresser as I straightened up.
Then I did it again.

"SARAH! DINNER'S READY!" Tommy yelled from the kitchen.

"I'll be right there!" I yelled back. But first I had to finish counting.

By the time I got downstairs, everyone was done eating. Tommy and Dad were clearing the table. Mom had run to the store. I didn't expect them to wait for me.

I made myself a plate and sat at the table by myself.

"Sorry I'm late."

"We missed you," Dad said.

"Do you want to hear a story I just made up?" I had been thinking about the OCD game.

"Sure."

"Once upon a time, there was a new teacher named Miss Brophy. On her first day of school, the other teachers welcomed her with a big plate of oatmeal cookies. 'Thank you,' Miss Brophy said. She invited the other teachers into her classroom and they ate the cookies together. She loved the oatmeal cookies, and she was so happy to make new friends. The teachers saw how much she liked the cookies, so the next day they brought her two plates of chocolate chip cookies, and the day after that they brought her three plates of banana bread. Miss

Brophy appreciated the gifts but was having trouble finishing them, so she nibbled and nibbled all day long until they were finally gone. Then the next day they brought her four plates of brownies. After that they brought her five plates of blueberry muffins. 'Whoa, that's too much!' Miss Brophy thought. But she kept on eating and eating because she didn't want to hurt their feelings. By Saturday she had a stomachache. The weekend was a nice break from all the sweets. 'Maybe they'll stop bringing them,' she hoped. On Monday, when she didn't see them coming, she felt relieved. But then there was a knock on her door..."

"More sweets?" Dad asked.

"You guessed it. A truckload of donuts."

"Jackpot!" Tommy said.

"But she didn't want any more!" I explained. "Enough is enough!"

"Boy, they really wore out their welcome," Dad said. "So what did she do?"

"She thanked them, but gave the donuts back. 'At first I liked the sweets, but then they gave me a stomachache, so now I'm eating healthier foods,' she told them."

"Oh, brother! I'd take the donuts," Tommy said.

"OCD's like that. At first it helped me feel better to count, but then something happened. The more I counted, the more I got the urges to count and then I ended up counting all the time! And it just made me feel worse."

"It wore out its welcome, too," Dad agreed.

We talked about the OCD game, how my obsessions and compulsions needed each other to play. So if I wanted to stop playing, then I would have to resist the urge to count and wait until it went away.

"I know you can do it," Dad said. "You can handle your fears without counting."

"I'm starting to think I can too, Dad." It felt good to say it out loud.

CHAPTER TWELVE
Resisting the Urge

Dear Diary,

Wow! I did it!
I really did it!!

I had an urge to open and close my closet door, and I resisted it!!! It turns out I was stronger than the urge! Who knew?? I feel brave. Now I just have to keep it up!! Wish me luck!!

P.S. My favorite thing in the world is when I'm waiting for the obsession and urge to go away and all of a sudden I realize they're gone! It's like, "Hey, I'm thinking about something totally different!" That's so awesome!

I was getting ready for school in the morning when the thought popped into my mind: "What if Mom died?" It would be so sad. I was feeling as if it were really going to happen, as if Mom's life were really in danger. I wanted to feel better, so I got the usual urge to open and close my closet door. I talked back to the urge and said, "No, I'm not playing the OCD game today!" I felt nervous, the way I always felt before I counted.

Just then, Lucky wandered into my room. "Good morning, kitty!" I said, as he rubbed his head on my leg and jumped onto the bed for a nap.

My anxiety rose like a wave in the ocean. I was prepared for that to happen, but I didn't realize how hard it would be to try and ignore it. I picked my dirty clothes up off the floor, put away my clean clothes, and put my lunch money in my pocket before I forgot. The urge was still there, distracting me, telling me to count...or I'd be sorry. I felt upset. My body was hot and sweaty. I sat on my bed and waited for it to go away.

"Can I do this?" I started to doubt myself. "What if mom died because I didn't open and close the closet door?" I didn't know if I could wait it out.

"Maybe I'll just open and close my door two times really quick," I thought.

"No, stick with it! It's just my OCD!" I reminded myself. "Mom's not really in danger." I called to Mom and she sat with me for a while. "Mom can take care of herself," I thought.

I brushed my teeth, then sat on the edge of the bed and petted Lucky for a while. "I'm the boss now, not OCD," I told him. And I waited some more.

Then, something strange happened. I didn't feel as nervous anymore. The urge to count was fading too! I realized I wasn't even thinking about the closet door as much, or Mom. I was thinking about the skirt I was learning to sew. The wave must be crashing, just like Dr. Goode said it would!

"Everything is okay," I thought to myself.

"Sarah, your bus is here," Mom called from the hallway.

"It's going to be fine," I realized. I grabbed my bag and kissed Lucky.

"You did it!" Mom said. It was true. I beat the urge for the first time! I smiled my biggest smile ever and ran to catch the bus.

CHAPTER THIRTEEN
In the Driver's Seat

Dear Diary,

I didn't open and close my closet door all week (well, Thursday I did a couple of times, but that's still good), and I didn't miss my bus once!!!! It's getting easier to resist my urges. Next week I'm going to work on not worrying about how many steps I take to the front door. Even if I take seven or nine steps (odd numbers), it'll be okay. I know nothing bad will happen, like I used to think. I feel lighter.

My obsessions are still there, but they're not as clingy and it's getting easier to let them go or turn down the volume on them. "A thought is just a thought," as Dr. Goode always says.

Kaelyn and I went back to WildWorld last weekend. When we got in line for the Python, I started worrying about Mom again, just

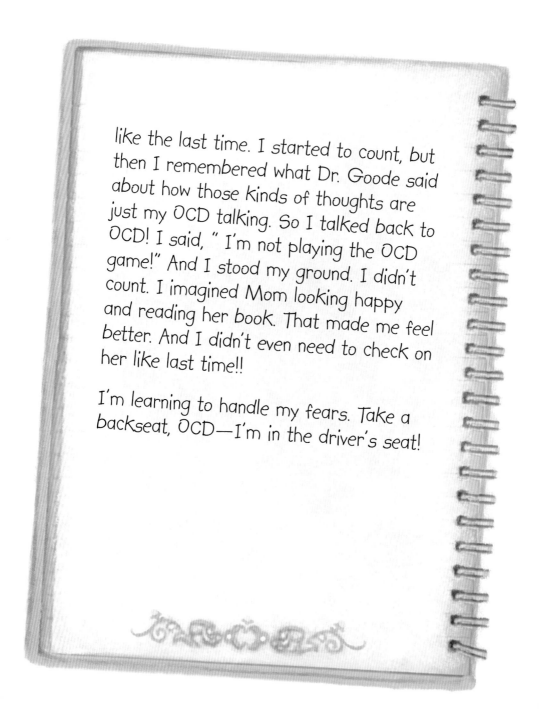

like the last time. I started to count, but then I remembered what Dr. Goode said about how those kinds of thoughts are just my OCD talking. So I talked back to OCD! I said, " I'm not playing the OCD game!" And I stood my ground. I didn't count. I imagined Mom looking happy and reading her book. That made me feel better. And I didn't even need to check on her like last time!!

I'm learning to handle my fears. Take a backseat, OCD—I'm in the driver's seat!

"Mom, do you remember the story I told you about the king?"

"Yes, the one who made up all those rules to protect his kingdom, like walking backwards on Wednesday, acting like monkeys on Monday...and what else?"

"Collecting ten turtles on Tuesday, never stepping on thorns on Thursday, and finding five fireflies on Friday," I reminded her. "Well, I thought of a different ending. If everyone stopped following the silly rules, it would show the king that they really didn't do any good."

"Good idea," Mom said.

"So when Tuesday came, they didn't collect the turtles. The king shouted, 'I need turtles!' But his subjects wouldn't look for any, and they wouldn't give in."

"Did anything bad happen?" Mom asked.

"No, everything was fine. Then, the next day, the people didn't walk backwards. And still, nothing bad happened. And then on Friday, nobody looked for fireflies either. And still, nothing bad happened. So that's when the king started to realize, 'Hey, maybe I'm not in danger all the time after all.'"

"That's great. So what did he do next?" Mom asked.

"He realized the silly rules were useless, so he got rid of them. He made a new royal proclamation: 'From now on, everyone can walk forward on

Wednesdays. We don't have to act like monkeys on Mondays either, and we can leave the turtles and fireflies alone!' And the people cheered.

"'Can we step on thorns on Thursdays?' they asked.

"'If you really, really want to, you can!' the king said. And everyone laughed.

"The king finally realized he could handle his fears, and he stopped thinking about his kingdom falling apart all the time."

"That sounds like someone else I know," Mom said wryly.

"Very good, Mother! Anyway, the king thanked everyone because he was finally free to do other things, like play polo and help people."

"All the things that kings do. That's a great ending," Mom said.

I had to agree.

Note to Readers

In *Ten Turtles on Tuesday,* Sarah has thoughts about something bad happening to her mom. These thoughts scare Sarah, and she counts to prevent something bad from happening to her mom. Counting makes her feel better at first, but it becomes a big problem over time. If you have obsessive-compulsive disorder, or OCD, like Sarah, the good news is that there are things you can do to beat it. Lots of other kids with OCD have overcome their OCD and so can you!

What Does the D in OCD Mean?

You probably know that OCD stands for obsessive-compulsive disorder. Obsessions are the thoughts, images, or doubts that bother and scare you. Compulsions are the things you do and think to decrease your fear and discomfort. Obsessions and compulsions are upsetting enough, but for some kids, the D in OCD can be pretty upsetting too. So what does the D in OCD mean anyway? One way to think of it is that the big D ("Disorder") is made up of four little d's that are making your life hard.

Disproportionate. The first little d, "disproportionate," just means that what you think and what you do are a bit over the top. Washing your hands quickly after you use the toilet makes good sense. Washing your hands over and over after you use the toilet and then taking a long shower because you still feel like you may have germs on your body doesn't make good sense. In fact, it doesn't make much sense at all, but you feel like you have to do it, which can be both scary and frustrating.

Disruptive. This means that your obsessions and compulsions are making it really hard for you to do the things you want to do in the way you want to do them. You may have trouble concentrating on your schoolwork because your mind is filled with all those scary obsessions. Even though you like school, you may hate going to school in the morning because of all the compulsions you have to do in order to start the day right. You may spend too much time washing, checking, or counting, making you late to the things you want to do. It's frustrating for you and for your family.

Distressing. This means that your obsessions and compulsions are really bothering you. Obsessions are not little worries. In fact, they're not worries at all. Worries kind of make sense. You might worry that if you don't get a good grade on your math test your mom and dad will be a little disappointed. But to think that if you don't get a good grade on your math test your mom and dad will get sick and die...well, that doesn't make sense at all. So, obsessions are very upsetting thoughts that don't make much sense when you step back and look at them. However, some kids have obsessions that don't scare them, but just make them feel uncomfortable or "not quite right." These kids will still do compulsions to relieve their discomfort, but if you ask them if they're afraid, they'll probably say, "No, I just don't feel right." Compulsions can be distressing too, and if your obsessions are scary or upsetting or even really uncomfortable, you'll have a lot of trouble resisting your compulsions, even if they don't make much sense. Although you don't have to have obsessions that are both *distressing* and *disruptive* to have the big D—just one will do it—most kids who want help for their OCD have both.

Duration. This just means that the other little d's (disproportionate, distressing, disruptive) have been pushing you around for longer than just a few days or weeks. Usually, if you've been suffering for more than six months, you may have this last little d.

So, that's all the D means in OCD—the O and C are bigger than you can handle on your own. That's where your family and the right therapist can help. Therapy helps get the D out of your life—even if a little O and C stick around—so that you can get back on track doing the things that are important to you. A little O and C never held back any kid. It's the D that does that.

You're Not Alone

No matter how scary the thought, how bad the thought, or how uncomfortable or guilty a thought makes you feel, other kids with OCD have had thoughts like that too. In fact, even kids without OCD sometimes have really strange and scary thoughts.

One of the hardest things about having OCD is that you may believe that you're all alone. You may think you're the only kid who has scary thoughts or does things that don't make sense. But you're not. One percent of kids have OCD. One percent may sound like a small number, but it's not. How many kids go to your school? If you're in elementary school, there may be 300–400 kids. Middle schools might have 600–700 kids. Many high schools have 700–800 kids. This means that if you're in elementary school, there are two or three other kids in your school with OCD. If you're in middle school, there may be six or seven, and if you're in high school, there may be seven or eight kids with OCD. Now think about all the schools in your city. Now think about all the schools in your state and then think about all the schools in the United States. That's a lot of schools and that's a lot of kids with OCD. Now, you might ask, "If there are so many other kids with OCD in my school, why don't I know them?" Well, you may not know them because they might be too embarrassed or too scared to tell you that they have OCD, too. But just because you don't know who they are doesn't mean that they're not there.

Turning OCD on Its Head

OCD has made your life hard by fooling you into thinking and acting in certain ways. As long as you continue to think and act in these ways, OCD is in charge. However, you can start to turn OCD on its head by trying a few simple things. These things might not help you completely overcome your OCD, but they're a good place to start.

Don't try to control your thoughts. Many kids (and adults too) believe that they can control their thoughts. They believe that they can think about what they want to think about, and more importantly, *not think* about what they don't want to think about. This isn't really true, however.

Try this. Close your eyes and think about polka-dotted zebras. Let them prance around in your mind. Now, try *not to think* about polka-dotted zebras. Try to keep them out of your mind. Don't try to think about something else in order to do this. That's controlling your attention, not your thoughts. Just try not to think about polka-dotted zebras by keeping your mind blank. Try very hard. Really push hard to keep polka-dotted zebras out of your mind.

What did you discover? Yep. There they are. This proves that we cannot control our thoughts, really, and if polka-dotted zebras really scared you, then keeping them out of your mind would be even harder. In fact, trying *not to think* about something only makes us think about it more because, in part, we're checking to see if we're thinking about it. And, guess what? Just as soon as we check whether we're thinking about something, sure enough, we start thinking about it.

So what can you do instead? Next time you're out with your family or a friend and an obsession enters your mind, try singing the obsession to a silly tune. For example, if you're afraid that you'll touch something and get sick, make up your own lyrics and sing it to yourself, perhaps to the tune of a favorite song. For example, to the tune of "Mary had a Little Lamb," sing something like, "Today, today, I might get sick. Might get sick. Might get sick. Today, today I might get sick and that is what I fear." What do you notice? Yep, it's tough not to giggle while singing a ridiculous song like that. That's the point. It's tough to be afraid of something that makes us laugh. You can try this in other ways too. You can speak the obsession in the voice of your favorite cartoon character. For example, Bugs Bunny, Daffy Duck, and Elmer Fudd are funny characters, but you probably have your own favorites. Say the obsession in a squeaky voice or a really low one, like Darth Vader. If you giggle, you win.

Negotiate with your compulsions, not with your obsessions. Sometimes it's not easy to tell the difference between an obsession, which is in your head, and a compulsion, which can be something you do but can also be something you think. For example, some kids reassure themselves. They think, "There's no way this would happen. No way!" You may feel a little better for a while, but this relief won't last. While it's true that the scary predictions are very, very, very unlikely to come true, OCD will always say to you, "Yes, but are you 100 percent certain? Are you totally sure?" Then you're anxious once again. You can never win an argument with OCD because you can never be certain. You can only be mostly and very nearly certain, but never absolutely certain, as in, "No way this will ever happen" certain. Some kids try to negotiate with their obsessions.

76

They think, "Well, if I wash my hands six times, and make certain I washed thoroughly, then that should be enough. Right?" Then OCD says to you, "Yes, but are you certain— really and truly certain it's enough?" You can't reason or negotiate with your obsessions. The obsessions always win.

You *can* negotiate with your compulsions, however. You can negotiate how much time you wash, how many times you check, how many times you do the same thing again and again. You can negotiate a delay that helps you resist doing the compulsion until the urge to do the compulsion fades and goes away. Then you win!

Try this. Next time OCD tells you to wash your hands or check the door, ask yourself, "How long can I delay doing the compulsion?" Can you delay for 5 minutes, 10 minutes, 30 minutes? Set a goal that you're confident you can achieve. Try to be at least 90 percent confident. For example, it may be really hard to delay washing your hands for the whole day but how about for 30 minutes? How about for 10 minutes?

The longer the delay, the less confident you'll feel that you can win against OCD. The shorter the delay, the more confident you'll feel. So, if you're 90 percent confident that you can delay washing for 10 minutes, then delay for 10 minutes. At the end of those 10 minutes, negotiate another delay with the compulsion. Perhaps you can delay another 10 minutes. Perhaps only 5 minutes this time. But 10 minutes and 5 minutes is a total delay of 15 minutes, and that might just be enough to win against OCD.

Negotiating with your compulsions is okay. It will help. Negotiating with your obsessions, on the other hand, will only make your OCD worse.

Bend and break OCD rules. Rules, rules, rules. That's OCD. Wash six times. Turn the faucet on and off twelve times. Walk a certain way. Think a certain way. You can free yourself from these OCD rules, however, a little at a time. Have you noticed what happens when you bend a paper clip back and forth? After a while, it breaks. Bending an OCD rule is the first step toward breaking an OCD rule altogether.

When OCD tells you to wash in a particular way—such as washing each finger one at a time, beginning with your little finger—bend the rule a little. Start with your thumb. Wash that first. This will make you a little uncomfortable, but continue to bend the OCD rule this way until bending this rule gets easy. Then, bend the rule in a different way. Perhaps wash your thumb first and then go back to the little finger and then to the thumb again. It doesn't matter how you bend the OCD rule. If it makes you a little uncomfortable, it's working. Bend the OCD rule until you're able to break it and stop doing it altogether. If OCD tells you to always start walking with your right foot, try starting with your left. If OCD tells you to read every single word on a page, try skipping one word per sentence or one word per paragraph. Remember, if it makes you a little uncomfortable, it's working. You're winning!

Step toward discomfort. Perhaps the most important thing you can do to turn OCD on its head is to practice stepping toward—rather than away from—discomfort every day. Stepping toward discomfort means that you no longer search for quick ways to escape your discomfort. Instead, you look for little ways to increase your discomfort, such as running your fingers along a dusty windowsill or scanning the newspaper for an article on a topic that, in the past, you would have avoided reading. Seeing discomfort as an opportunity rather than a burden will help you stay on top of your OCD each day.

Don't be afraid to ask for help. As you've learned, one of the ways OCD stays in charge is by convincing you that your obsessions and compulsions are horrible and terrible—a big secret that you cannot share with anyone. Reading this book is a great first step in turning OCD on its head and breaking free from the frustration and embarrassment that OCD has caused you. However, if after reading the book and trying a few things, you're still having a hard time, talk to your parent or another trusted adult about getting more help. They can arrange for you to speak to a professional therapist who will know other ways to help you turn OCD on its head.

Remember, you're not alone. No matter what you're thinking or doing, other kids have thought those things and done those things before. Furthermore, with the right help, you too can not only turn OCD on its head, but also make it do back flips. Then you're really in charge. Good luck!

Michael Tompkins, PhD, is a licensed psychologist who specializes in cognitive–behavior therapy for anxiety disorders in adults, adolescents, and children. Dr. Tompkins is the author or co-author of six books, including the Magination Press book *My Anxious Mind: A Teen's Guide to Managing Anxiety and Panic,* co-authored with Katherine Martinez, PsyD.

About the Author

Ellen Flanagan Burns is a school psychologist and the author of *Nobody's Perfect: A Story for Children About Perfectionism*. She devotes her writing to helping children overcome anxiety. She believes that children's books can be a powerful therapeutic tool and supports cognitive-based interventions for children with anxiety-related issues. Ms. Burns lives in Newark, Delaware with her family, where she is also a practicing licensed massage therapist.

About the Illustrator

Sue Cornelison has loved to draw since she was young. Now that she is grown, Sue illustrates in her "Tree Top" art studio in her backyard in rural Iowa. Together with husband, Ross, she raised six children. When she is not drawing and painting, she coaches trampoline and tumbling and feels blessed to be in her element. Past projects include *Sofia's Dream, You're Wearing That to School!?*, the award-winning "Howard B. Wigglebottom" series, and the "Bitty Baby" series for American Girl. She works in a variety of mediums, including digital and oil. *Ten Turtles on Tuesday* combined digital underpaintings with colored pencil on Strathmore 500 paper.

About Magination Press

Magination Press is an imprint of the American Psychological Association, the largest scientific and professional organization representing psychologists in the United States and the largest association of psychologists worldwide.

APPENDIX B

Gaspar de Porres. In this year only two *autos* were re[presented], both by Porres. For these he received 3[...] reals. (*Bull Hisp.* (1907), p. 372.)

Baltasar Pinedo and Juan de Morales Medrano.

Baltasar Pinedo and Nicolas de los Rios.

Alonso Riquelme and Juan de Morales Medrano.

Alonso de Heredia and Domingo Balbin.

Alonso Riquelme and Hernan Sanchez de Vargas.

Hernan Sanchez de Vargas and Tomas Fernandez d[e] Cabredo.

Juan de Morales Medrano and Tomas Fernandez de Cabredo.

Alonso de Riquelme and Antonio de Villegas.

Juan de Morales Medrano and Baltasar Pinedo. (*Bull. Hisp.* (1907), p. 379.)

Hernan Sanchez de Vargas and Pedro de Valdes.

Pedro Cebrian and Pedro Cerezo de Guevara. In Paz y Melia, *Catálogo,* No. 1641, we read that Alonso de Riquelme represented Lope's *auto La Isla del Sol* in this year.

Cristóbal de Leon and Baltasar Pinedo.

Baltasar Pinedo and Hernan Sanchez de Vargas.

Baltasar Pinedo and Hernan Sanchez de Vargas.

Alonso de Olmedo and Cristobal de Avendaño.

Pedro de Valdes and Cristobal de Avendaño. (*Bull. Hisp.* (1908), p. 244.)

Manuel Vallejo.

Juan de Morales Medrano and Antonio de Prado.

Juan de Morales Medrano and Antonio de Prado.

Andrés de la Vega, Tomas Fernandez de Cabredo, and Juan de Morales Medrano. In this year each *autor* represented one *auto* and a part of the fourth *auto.* (*Bull. Hisp.* (1908), p. 252.)

Cristobal de Avendaño and Andrés de la Vega.

Roque de Figueroa and Andrés de la Vega.

Andrés de la Vega and Bartolomé Romero.

Bartolomé Romero and Roque de Figueroa.

Andrés de la Vega and Roque de Figueroa.

Manuel Vallejo and Francisco Lopez.

APPENDIX A

Octubre.—2 á 30. Osorio.

Noviembre.—1 á 25. Osorio. 26 á 30. Cisneros.

Diciembre.—1° Cisneros. 2. Osorio. 3. Cisneros. 4 y 5. Cisneros. 6 y 7. Melchor de Leon. 8 á 15. Cisneros y Leon. 17. Cisneros y Osorio. 18 y 19. Leon y Cisneros. 20. Cisneros. 21. Leon y Cisneros. Trabajo tambien un *volador.* 23. Cisneros y Leon. 25. Cisneros. 26 y 27. Cisneros y Leon. 28. Leon. Hubo comedia en casa de Gonzalo de Monzon. 30. Cisneros y Leon.

Total de ingresos en el año 1590: 1,840,613 maravedís. Gastos: igual cantidad. (*Archivo de la Diputacion. Manual del Hospital general,* II, 158, 8.)

1601

Enero.—1° Gaspar de Porres y Baltasar Pinedo. 3 á 24. Porres y Pinedo. 25 y 26. Pinedo. 28, 30 y 31. Porres y Pinedo.

Febrero.—1° Porres y Diego Lopez de Alcaraz. 2. Porres y Pinedo. 3. Alcaraz. 4. Porres y Pinedo. 5 á 8. Porres y Alcaraz. 9. Pinedo y Alcaraz. 10. Porres y Pinedo. 11. Pinedo y Alcaraz. 13 á 16. Porres y Alcaraz. 17 y 18. Porres y Pinedo. 19. Porres y Alcaraz. 20. Porres y Pinedo. 21. Porres y Alcaraz. 22. Porres y Pinedo. 23 á 25. Pinedo y Alcaraz. 26 y 27. Porres y Pinedo. 28. Alcaraz y Pinedo.

Marzo.—1° Porres y Pinedo. 2. Porres y Alcaraz. 3. Pinedo y Alcaraz. 4. Porres y Pinedo. 5. Porres y Alcaraz. 6. Pinedo y Alcaraz.

Abril.—29 á 30. Gaspar de Porres.

Mayo.—1° á 7. Gaspar de Porres. 9. Pedro Jiménez de Valenzuela. 10 y 11. Porres y Gabriel Vaca. 12. Porres. 13 á 15. Porres y Vaca. 16. Vaca. 18. Porres. 19 á 22. Porres y Vaca. 23 á 31. Porres.

Junio.—3 á 17. Gaspar de Porres. 22. Porres (Autos en el teatro). 23 y 24. Autos á los semaneros en el teatro.

Julio.—12, 13, 18 y 22. Gabriel de la Torre. 23 y 30. Antonio de Villegas.

Agosto.—3 á 31. Villegas.

Septiembre.—3 á 30. Villegas.

Octubre.—2 á 18. Villegas.   19. Los *Franceses*.   20 y 21. Villegas.   26, 27 y 28. Gabriel de la Torre.

Noviembre.—2 á 13. Gabriel de la Torre.   14 á 23. Gabriel Vaca y Pedro Jiménez de Valenzuela [these two *autores* managed a company in partnership].

Diciembre.—2 á 18. Vaca y Jiménez de Valenzuela.   21 á 31. Villegas. (*Archivo de la Diputacion. Manual del Hospital general*, II, 158, 8.)

1602

Enero.—4 á 29. Jerónimo Lopez.

Abril.—8 y 9. Pedro Jiménez de Valenzuela.

Mayo.—3. Pedro Jiménez de Valenzuela.   23, 24. Los *Españoles* [this company was formed by Pedro Rodriguez, Diego de Rojas, and Gaspar de los Reyes].   26 á 28. Pedro Jiménez de Valenzuela.

Junio.—16 y 18. Los *Españoles*.

Agosto.—11 á 30. Villegas.

Septiembre.—3 á 30. Villegas.

Octubre.—1 á 9. Villegas.   31. Villegas.

Noviembre.—1 á 7. Antonio Granados.   8. Gabriel de la Torre.   10 á 27. Granados.

Diciembre.—4 á 29. Juan de Morales. (*Archivo de la Diputacion. Manual del Hospital general*, II, 198, 8.)

APPENDIX B

AUTORES DE COMEDIAS WHO REP[RESENTED]
AUTOS SACRAMENTALES IN [...]

1574   Jerónimo Velazquez represented thr[...] festival of this year.

1578   Alonso de Cisneros, three *autos*.

1579   Mateo de Salcedo.

1580   Alonso de Cisneros.

1581   Jerónimo Velazquez.

1582   Alonso de Cisneros and Jerónimo Ve[...]

1585   Gaspar de Porres, three *autos*.

1586   Jerónimo Velazquez represented three [...]

1587   Nicolas de los Rios, Miguel Ramirez, [...]

1589   Jerónimo Velazquez, three *autos*.

1590   Nicolas de los Rios and Alonso de Cis[...]

1591   Alonso de Cisneros.

1592   Gaspar de Porres and Rodrigo de Saa[...]

1593   Alonso de Cisneros and Gaspar de Por[...]

1594   Jerónimo Velazquez, two *autos*.

1595   Alonso de Cisneros and Antonio de Vi[...]

1596   Nicolas de los Rios and Antonio de Vil[...]

1597   Nicolas de los Rios.

1598   Antonio de Villegas and Diego Lopez [...]

1599   Gaspar de Porres (two *autos*); Dieg[...] and Luis de Vergara, each an *auto*.

1600   Melchor de Villalba and Gabriel de [...] *autos*.

1602   Pedro Jimenez de Valenzuela.

1603   Juan de Morales Medrano.

1604   Gaspar de Porres.

358
1605
1606
1607
1608
1609
1610
1611
1612
1613
1614
1615
1616
1617
1618
1619
1620
1621
1622
1623
1624
1625
1626
1627
1628
1629
1630
1632

1633 Antonio de Prado and Manuel Vallejo.
1637 Pedro de la Rosa and Tomas Fernandez de Cabredo.
1638 Bartolomé Romero (two *autos*) and Antonio de Rueda and
        Pedro Ascanio (each one).
1639 Antonio de Rueda and Manuel Vallejo.
1640 Bartolomé Romero.

APPENDIX C

CASTS OF COMEDIAS

The following casts of comedias of the seventeenth century have been collected from various sources, the most of them from manuscripts in the Biblioteca Nacional. They are arranged in chronological order.

La bella Ester (1610)

Lope de Vega. Autog. MS. in British Museum, dated at Madrid, April 5, 1610. This comedia was afterward published in Part XV of Lope's *Comedias* under the title *La hermosa Ester*.

Bassan	Morales
Egeo	Vicente
Tarses	Torres
Marsanes	Carrillo
Adamasa	Fuentes
Setar	Morales
El Rey Assuero	Sanchez
Un Capitan	Carrillo
Mardoqueo	Toledo
La Reyna Vasti	
Ester	Sᵃ Polonia
Selvagio	Vicente
Sirena, *labradora*	Clara
Musica	Villaverde
Aman	Rosales

In Act III the part of Marsanes is assigned to Antonio. This is the company of Hernan Sanchez de Vargas.

La buena Guarda ó la Encomienda bien guardada (1610)

Lope de Vega. Autog. MS. dated at Madrid, April 16, 1610,
formerly in the possession of the Marquis Pidal.

Personas del P° Acto:

Leonarda .... Catalina [de Valcázar]
Doña Luisa .... Mariana [de Herbias?]
Un Escudero .... [Martin de?] Vivar
Don Juan .... Luis
Don Luis .... [Pedro de] España
El hermano Carrizo, *sacristan* .... [Diego Lopez] Basurto
Felix, *mayordomo* .... [Alonso de] Olmedo
Doña Clara .... Maria de Argüello
Doña Elena .... Catalina
Don Pedro, *su padre* .... [Luis de] Quiñones
Ricardo, *viejo* .... España
Don Carlos ....Benito [de Castro]
Musicos ....

Hablan en el Segundo Acto:

Felix .... [Alonso de] Olmedo
Carrizo .... [Diego Lopez] Basurto
Doña Clara .... Maria de Argüello
Un Angel .... Mariana
Una Voz .... Catalina Valcacer
Portera ....
Don Carlos .... Benito [de Castro]
Ginés .... [Agustin] Coronel
Carrizo, *fingido* .... Vivar
Un pastor ....[Alonso de] Riquelme
Un huesped ....[Pedro de] Callenueva

Hablan en el 3° Acto:

Carrizo .... Basurto
Felix .... Olmedo
Tres bandoleros .... Coronel, España, Callenueva

Liseno ⎱ *villanos* .... Argüello
Cosme ⎰ .... Luis

Dos damas...................................⎰ Catalina
                                     ⎱ Jerónima

Dos galanes ....⎰ España
                                      ⎱ Luis

Dos musicos ....

Dos nadadores ....⎰ Vivar
                                      ⎱ Callenueva

Don Carlos .... Benito
Un pastor .... Riquelme
Un Angel .... Mariana
Don Pedro .... Quiñones
Ginés .... Coronel
La hortelana .... Jerónima
La portera .... Catalina
Carrizo, *fingido* .... Vivar
Un platero .... Callenueva

This is the company of Alonso Riquelme. *Comedias escogidas de Lope de Vega,* ed. Hartzenbusch (*Bibl. de Aut. Esp.*), Vol. III, p. 326.

La Discordia en los Casados (1611)

Lope de Vega. Autog. MS. (Osuna) dated at Madrid, August 2, 1611, with licenses to 1618. Paz y Melia, *Catálogo,* No. 933.

Alberto .... Arellano. Soria
Aurelio .... Quiñones
Musico .... Quiñones

Personas del 3° Acto:

Cenardo .... Arellano. Soria
Panfilo .... Herrera

El Bastardo Mudarra (1612)

Lope de Vega. Autog. MS. signed at Madrid, April 27, 1612, formerly in the possession of Sr. Olózaga. I have an excellent photo-zincograph of it, published in 1886.

Personas del P⁰ Acto:

Doña Alanbra .... Ana Maria
Gonzalo Bustos .... Cintor
Rui Velazquez .... Benito
Gonzalo Gonzalez .... Cintorico

The remaining characters are unassigned. The MS. contains licenses to represent dated Madrid, May 17, 1612; Çaragoça, January 29, 1613, and Antequera, May 13, 1616, and in 1617.

La Dama boba (1613)

Lope de Vega. Autog. MS. (Osuna) dated at Madrid, April 28, 1613. Paz y Melia, *Catálogo,* No. 810.

Liseo, *caballero* .... Ortiz [de Villazan]
Leandro, *caballero* .... Almonte
Turin, *lacayo* .... [Baltasar de?] Carvajal
Octavio, *viejo* .... [Luis de] Quiñones
Miseno, *su amigo* .... [Juan de] Villanueva
Duardo .... Guebara
Laurencio .... Benito [de Castro]
Feniso, *caballero* .... [Manuel] Simon
Rufino, *maestro* .... [Pedro] Aguado
Nise, *dama* .... Jeronima [de Burgos]
Finea, *su hermana* .... Maria [de los Angeles?]
Celia, *criada* .... Isabel [Rodriguez?]
Clara, *criada* .... Ana Maria [de Ribero]

This is the company of Pedro de Valdes. Perhaps the "Isabel" is Isabel de Velasco, who married Luis Quiñones in 1614.

La Tercera de la Sancta Juana (1614)

Tirso de Molina. Autog. MS. inedited [since published by Sr. Cotarelo], dated at Toledo, August 6, 1614. *Catálogo*, No. 3035. I have a copy of this MS. made years ago. The cast is in Tirso's hand. It was represented, apparently, by two companies. The characters of the play are in the middle column:

Bernardo .... Don Luis .... [Luis de] Toledo
[Iñigo de] Loaisa .... Çesar .... [Juan de] Montemayor
Diego .... Don Diego, *viejo* .... Cristobal
Nauarete .... Lillo ...... [Antonio de] Sanpayo
Xρo. nr͞o Sr. .... Montemayor
Mª .... La Sancta .... Mª de Morales
Lorenzo .... S. Laruel .... Antº de Prado
Ana Mª .... Aldonça . La Sª Petronila[de Loaysa]
Peynado, *pastor* .... [Pedro] Aguado
Isabel .... Doña Ines
La Sª Ana Maria[de Ulloa?]
Montemayor .... Crespo, *pastor* .... Aguado
Mingo, *pastor* ..[Cristobal de] S. Pedro
Berrueco *pastor* .... Juan Ximenez

2º Acto. Personas:

Don Luis .... Toledo
Aldonça .... la Sra Petronila
Don Diego .... S. Pedro
Lillo .... Sanpayo
D. Jorge .... Xρōbal
Maria, *monja* .... la Sra Anna Maria
Doña Ines .... la dicha
Çesar .... Montemayor
Nr͞a Señora .... la Sra Petronila
El niño Jesus .... Sanpaico
El Angel .... Antonio del Prado

3º Acto. Personas de el:

D. Diego .... Alonso fre. [Alonso Fernandez de Guardo?]
D. Luis .... Toledo

Lillo .... Sanpayo. Guardia
Crespo .... Aguado
Berrueco .... Juº Ximenez
Mingo .... S. Pº [i.e. San Pedro]
Çesar .... Mᵗᵉmayor
Doña Ynes .... Ana Cabello
La Santa .... Mᵃ de Morales
El Angel .... Antonio de Prado. Juan de Madrid
Nuestra Señora .... la Sᵃ Petronila [de Loaysa]
Jesus Niño .... Sanpaico
Maria, *monja* .... la Sᵃ Ana Maria
Otra monja .... la Sᵃ Madalena [de Oviedo]
Una niña .... Sanpaico
Un Alma .... Juº Ximenez

En Toledo, a 24 de Agosto de 1614 años.

El Sembrar en buena Tierra (1616)

Lope de Vega. Autog. MS. in British Museum, dated Madrid, January 6, 1616. It contains a license to perform, signed by Tomas Gracian Dantisco on January 12, 1616.

Personas del Pº Acto:

Don Felix .... [Cristobal] Ortiz [de Villazan]
Florencio .... Benito
Galindo, *criado* .... Sanchez
Doña Prudencia .... Eugenia [de Villegas?]
Ynes ....
Celia .... Luçia
Elena ....
Fabio .... [Francisco Muñoz de la] Plaza
Felino .... [Antonio] Ramos
Don Alonso .... [Juan de] Valdivieso
Lizardo .... Herrera
Liseo .... Escruela[?]
Fidelio .... Rā

Personas del 2º Acto:

Arseno .... Ceruela
Otavio .... Ramon
Un escriuano .... Ramos
Un alguacil .... Plaza

The other characters are unassigned.

3º Acto:

Florencio .... Benito

The name of one of these actors once appears as Escruela, then as Ceruela. This name is otherwise unknown. Escoriguela was a well-known player.

Quien mas no puede (1616)

Lope de Vega. Autog. MS. dated at Madrid, September 1, 1616, in the possession of Mr. John Murray.

Personas del Pº Acto:

Ramiro, *Rey de Nauarra* .... Zancado
Don Beltran, *criado suyo* .... Bernardino
El Conde Henrriq̄ .... Xρōbal
Nuño, *criado del Conde* .... Ossorio
Doña Eluira, *ynfanta* .... Ana
Lucinda, *donzella suya* .... Francisca
Ordoño, *Rey de Leon* .... Pº Zebrian
Laynez, *criado del Rey* .... Cuebas
Yñigo, *criado del Conde* .... el q̄ bayla, Alº
Doña Blanca, *hermᵃ del Conde* .... Maritardia

Personas del 2º Acto:

Doña Blanca ....
Don Yñigo ....
Celio .... Antonio
Laynez ....
Don Sancho .... Cuebas

Don Arias .... Antonio
Lisis .... Francisca o Ana Muñoz
Riselo .... o Cuebas o Bernardino
Menandro Villanas .... el q̄ bayle q̄ no se el nonbre

Luzinda, El Conde Henrriq̄, Doña. Eluira, Nuño, Rey Ramiro, Don Beltran, unassigned. In the third act only one character is assigned: Estela to Francisca.

Las Paredes oyen· (1617)

Juan Ruiz de Alarcon. D. Luis Fernandez Guerra, *D. Juan Ruiz de Alarcon,* Madrid, 1871, p. 257, says that the MS., apparently an autograph, is preserved in the Osuna library. But between this date and 1882, when Rocamora published his Catalogue of the Osuna manuscripts, it must have disappeared, for it is not mentioned by Rocamora and never passed into the possession of the Biblioteca Nacional. See *ibid.,* p. 497.

Celia .... Dorotea [de Sierra]
D. Juan .... [Damian] Arias
Beltran .... Pedro de Villegas
Doña Ana .... Maria de Cordoba
Ortiz .... Frasquito
D. Mendo .... [Luis Bernardo de] Bobadilla
Lucrecia .... Maria de Vitoria
Conde .... Azua
Duque .... [Gabriel] Cintor
Escudero .... ·
Marcelo .... ·
Leonido .... Francisco de Robles
Un arriero .... Bernardino [Alvarez?]
Una musica .... Maria de Vitoria
Otro musico .... [Juan] Mazana
Otro musico .... Navarrete

La Guarda cuidadosa

Miguel Sanchez, *el Divino.* The comedia was first printed at Alcalá in 1615. The manuscript from which the following cast is taken, and which was formerly in the Osuna collection, is now in the Biblioteca Nacional. Paz y Melia, *Catálogo,* No. 1431. It is of the early seventeenth century. See *La Isla barbara* and *La Guarda cuidadosa,* two comedies by Miguel Sanchez (*el Divino*), ed. by H. A. Rennert, Boston and Halle, 1896.

Trebacio .... Lorenzo [Hurtado?]
Leucato .... Diego
Príncipe .... [Juan de] Montemayor
Roberto .... [Iñigo de] Loaysa
Nisea .... Maria [de Jesus? de Vitoria?]
Arsinda .... Ana Maria [de Ulloa?]
Florela, *labradora* .... Isabelica
Ariadeno .... Navarrete
Fileno .... Miñano
Florencio .... Bernardo

In a MS. comedia of the beginning of the seventeenth century, *Como a de usarse del Bien y a de preuenirse el Mal,* existing in the Biblioteca Palatina at Parma and described by Professor Restori in *Studj di Filologia Romanza,* fasc. 15, Roma, 1891, p. 129, occur the names of the following players: Sotomayor, Olmedo(?), Isabelica, Naba[rrete], La Sᵃ Bernarda, Tapia, Perez, and Loaysa. This comedia, which was afterward published (Halle, 1899) by Professor Restori with the title:

Los Guzmanes de Toral,

was written by Lope de Vega, and, as the title occurs in the first list of his *Peregrino en su Patria,* is prior to 1604. The third act is in Lope's hand and has the following cast:

Rey Don Alfonso .... Sotomayor
Doña Greida .... Mᵃ
Don Payo .... Obredo [Olmedo?]
Doña Aldonza .... Isabelica
Tirso .... Trebiño
Godinez, *lacayo* .... Naba[rrete]
Urgel .... Diego
Alvaro .... Olmedo

Pascuala .... la Sᵃ Bernarda
Doña Ana de Haro .... Isabel bᵃ
Don Garcia ....
Don Lope Diaz de Haro .... Diego
Sancho Manrique .... Diego
Verveco .... Tapia
Mireno .... Juanico
Soldado 1º .... Tapia
Soldado 2º .... Juanico
Soldado 3º .... Perez
Alonso Ansurez .... Loaisa

El Desden vengado (1617)

Lope de Vega. Autog. MS. signed at Madrid, August 4, 1617, formerly in the Osuna library, now in the Biblioteca Nacional. Paz y Melia, *Catálogo*, No. 871.

El Conde Lucindo .... Fadrique
Tomin, *criado* .... [Agustin] Coronel
Feniso .... Juan Jeronimo [Valenciano]
Roberto, *caballero* .... Juan de Vargas
Leonardo .... Cosme
Rugero, *Rey de Napoles* .... Juan Bautista [Valenciano]
Lisena, *dama* .... Dᵃ Maria [Coronel?]
Celia, *dama* .... Manuela [Enriquez]
Evandro, *su padre* ....
Ynarda, *criada* .... Vincenta [de Borja?]

Schack, *Nachträge,*. p. 46. This is probably the company of Juan Bautista Valenciano.

El Martir de Madrid (1619)

Mira de Amescua. Partly autograph, with a license to perform dated 1619. Paz y Melia, *Catálogo*, No. 2029. There are other licenses as late as 1641.

Alvaro Ramirez .... Jusepe
D. Fernando .... Lorenzo [Hurtado] el autor

La infelice Dorotea (1620)

Andres de Claramonte wrote it for Juan Bautista Valenciano. Sanchez-Arjona, *Anales del Teatro en Sevilla*, p. 214. MS. copy in the Biblioteca Nacional. Paz y Melia, *Catálogo*, No. 1594.

D. Garcinuñez .... Fadrique
El Rey .... Juan Jerónimo [Valenciano]
D. Fernando .... Juan Bautista [Valenciano]
Nuño de Lemos .... Andres [de Claramonte?]
Arnao .... [Agustin] Coronel
Solano .... Miguel
Layn .... [Cristobal de?] Avendaño
Mendo .... Jusepe
Teodora .... Sª Maria [Candau?]
Dorotea .... Sª Manuela [Enriquez]
Leonor .... Sra Maria de los Angeles
D. Juan .... Manuel de Coca

Amor, Pleito y Desafío (1621)

Lope de Vega. Autog. MS. dated at Madrid, November 23, 1621, with a license of January 14, 1622. Formerly in the Durán collection and now in the Biblioteca Nacional. *Catálogo*, No. 171.

D. Alvaro de Rojas .... [Pedro] Maldonado
D. Juan de Padilla .... Lorenzo Hurtado
D. Juan de Aragon .... Francisco Triviño
El Rey Alfonso .... Juan Bautista [Valenciano]
Doña Beatriz .... la Señora Angela [de Toledo?]
Dª Ana .... la Sra Francisca de Soria(?)
Martin, *escudero* .... Antonio Rodriguez
Tello, *criado* .... Vicente
Sancho, *criado* .... Pedro de Valdes
Leonor .... la Señora Jeronima [de Burgos]

La nueva Victoria de D. Gonzalo de Cordoba (1622)

Lope de Vega. Autog. MS. in the Biblioteca Nacional, dated at Madrid, October 8, 1622. *Catálogo,* No. 2409.

Lisarda, *dama* .... la S^{ra} Manuela [Enriquez]
Fulgencia, *criada* .... S^{ra} Ana
D. Juan Ramirez .... Fadrique
Bernabé, *lacayo* .... [Agustin] Coronel
El Capitan Medrano .... Cosme
Estevan, *criado* .... Jusepe
El Bastardo .... Juan Jeronimo [Valenciano]
El Obispo de Holstad .... [Juan de] Vargas
El Duque de Bullon .... Jusepe
D. Gonzalo de Cordoba .... Juan Bautista [Valenciano]
D. Francisco de Harras .... Manuel
El Baron de Tili .... Naruaez
Musico .... [Manuel] Simon

El Poder en el Discreto (1623)

Lope de Vega. Autog. MS. in the Biblioteca Nacional, dated at Madrid, May 8, 1623. Paz y Melia, *Catálogo,* No. 2649. There are two casts given in the MS.

Serafina, *dama* .... Maria Calderon ...... Josefa [Vaca?]
Rosela, *criada* .... Dª Isabel ....
Teodosio, *Rey de Sicilia* ... Lezcano .... Bracamonte
Celio, *de su camara* .... Morales .... Arias
Alejo, *criado de Celio* ..... Castro .... Triviño
El Conde de Augusta ..... Suarez .... Morales
Flora, *dama* .... Mariana [Vaca] .... Mariana [Vaca]

The MS. contains a license dated 1624, and the company on the right was in all probability that of Juan de Morales Medrano, in which both his wife and his daughter Mariana appeared. My copy gives the name "Bracamonte," not Vacamonte.

Celos con Celos se curan (1625)

Tirso de Molina. MS. copy, formerly in the Osuna collection, now in the Biblioteca Nacional. Paz y Melia, *Cátalogo*, No. 563. It contains licenses dated 1625. There are two casts:

Çesar	[Cristobal] de Avendaño	Gutierrez
Carlos	Viera	Segobia
Gascon	Bernardo	Matias
Sirena	Maria de Montesinos	Juana de los Reyes
Diana	Catalina Moreno	Ines
Marco Antonio	Lezcano	Francisco Alonso
Alejandro	[?]	Juan Alonso
Narcisa	Mª Candau	Luisa
Un grande chico	[Balt.] Moreno	[?]
Un jardinero	Ordoñez	Marcos

The first of these companies seems to be that of Cristóbal de Avendaño about the year 1632.

El Brasil restituido (1625)

Lope de Vega. Autog. MS. dated at Madrid, October 23, 1625, now in the Lenox Library, New York.

Personas del Pº Acto:

Doña Guiomar	Mª de Vitoria
Don Diego	[Gabriel?] Cintor
Bernardo	Bernardino [Alvarez?]
Laurencio	[Juan] Antonio
Leonardo	[Luis Bernardo de] Bobadilla
El Coronel de Olanda	Arias con barba Françesa
Alberto, *su hijo*	El Spir santo del Auto
El Gobernador	El Autor
Machado	Pedro [de Villegas?]
La Monarquia de España	
Ongol	
Darin	
Soldados	
El Brasil	Maria de Cordoba

Personas del 2º Acto:

La religion Catolica .... Dorotea [de Sierra]
El Brasil .... La Autora
D. Manuel de Meneses .... Musico
D. Fadrique de Toledo .... Arias
Leonardo .... Bobadilla
Machado .... Pedro
Dª Guiomar .... Mª de Vitoria
D. Juan de Orellana .... [Juan] Mazana
D. Diego Ramirez ....
El Coronel electo .... Bernardino
Don Enrique de Alagon .... Cintor
Don Diego de Espinosa .... Antonio
Don Pedro de Santisteban .... frᶜᵒ de rro [Francisco de Robles?]
Apolo .... Arias
La heregia .... Mª de Vitoria
Un soldado .... el niño

This is probably the company of Andres de la Vega. See my article in the *Mod. Lang. Review* for January, 1906, p. 108.

El piadoso Aragones (1626)

Lope de Vega. Autog. MS. dated at Madrid, August 17, 1626, now in the Biblioteca Nacional. Paz y Melia, *Catálogo,* No. 2607. Licenses of Madrid, September 15, 1626; Zaragoza, 1627, and Lisbon, 1631.

Almirante .... Vicente
D. Bernardo .... [Pedro?] Jordan
D. Pedro Agramonte .... Quadrado
Alcalde .... Lorenzo

These names are crossed out, and the following are added:

D. Pedro Agramonte .... Felipe
Bernardo .... Jordan
Raymundo de Luna .... Mateo
Mendoza .... Tapia

Musico .... Leon
D. Juan de Beamonte .... Max°

El Favor en la Sentencia (1626)

Jacinto Cordeiro. Autog. MS. in the Biblioteca Nacional. Paz
y Melia, *Catálogo*, No. 1242. Written for Bartolomé Romero.

Porcia .... la Autora [Antonia Manuela Catalan]
Arminda .... Dorotea
Rey .... Estrada[?]
El Principe .... [Gabriel] Zintor
Conde .... [Alonso de] Osuna
Rosando .... Autor [Bartolome Romero]
Dᵃ Linda .... Micaela
Gascon .... Tomas [Enriquez?]

Sanchez-Arjona, *Anales*, p. 272.

Amor con vista (1626)

Lope de Vega. Autog. MS. signed at Madrid on December 10,
1626. Licenses to perform in Madrid, of 1627, and in Lisbon,
1630. In the Biblioteca Nacional. Paz y Melia, *Catálogo*, No.
149.
El Conde Otabio .... Autor [Antonio de Prado]
Tome, *criado suyo* .... [Luis Bernardo de] Bobadilla
Celia .... Mᵃ de Calderon [this is crossed out] Vitoria
Lisena .... Autora [Mariana Vaca de Morales]

2° Acto:
Julio .... Jeronimo

Sin Secreto no ay Amor (1626)

Lope de Vega. Autog. MS. signed at Madrid, July 18, 1626,
with licenses to perform of Madrid, August 2, 1626; Zaragoza,
October 13, 1626, and Granada, April 28, 1630. British Museum.
Published by me, Baltimore, 1894 (Mod. Lang. Assoc.).
Celio .... Tapia
Fabricio .... Jeronimo

Del Monte sale quien el Monte quema (1627)

Lope de Vega. Autog. MS. signed at Madrid, October 20, 1627. Licenses of Madrid, May 17, 1628; Valencia, September 28, 1628; Granada, October 1, 1636. In the Biblioteca Nacional. *Catálogo*, No. 848.

El Conde Henrrique	Arias
Feliciano	Jusepe
Narcisa, *labradora*	Sᵃ Maria de Heredia
Tirso, *villano*	Heredia
Juana, *labradora*	Sᵃ Catalina [de Medina?]
Celia, *dama*	Sᵃ Ana Maria [de Ulloa?]
Clara, *criada*	Sᵃ Francisca
El Rey de Francia	[Francisco de] Salas
Mauricio, *Gobernador*	[Juan de] Montemayor
El Marques Roselo	Sʳ Marcos. Rueda
Leonelo, *Capitan*	Alvarez

The names Valdes, Mencos, and Francisca also occur.

La Conpetencia en los Nobles (1628?)

Lope de Vega. MS. in the British Museum with corrections supposed to be in the hand of Lope.

Acto 2º:

D. Juan	[Juan] Antonio
D. Pedro	[Manuel] Simon
Hernando	Autor
Guzman	Canobas
Don Luis	Damian [Arias?]
Don Diego	Luis de Salaçar
El Rey	Nabarrete
Beltran	Saçedo
Doña Juana	Ana de Moya
Doña Maria	Catalina [de Peralta?]
Leonor	su muger de Nabarrete
Toreadores	Marcos y Grajales

According to the *suelta* of this comedia, it was first represented by Tomas Fernandez. It was in the repertory of the companies of Rueda and Ascanio in 1638–40. See Rosell, *Entremeses de Benavente,* Vol. I, p. 377.

La gran Columna fogosa (1629?)

Lope de Vega. MS. copy in Biblioteca Nacional. Paz y Melia, *Catálogo,* No. 1412. The MS. contains original licenses dated at Plasencia, 1629.

El Enperador Valente, *ereje* .... Al⁰ Gomez
Pretoriano, *ereje* .... P⁰ Gonçalez
Agustulo, *ereje* .... Dominguez
Posidonio, *ereje* .... Domingo Hernandez
San Basio, *Obispo* .... Fernando Lopez
Eraclio, *cauallero biejo* .... Gaspar Serrano
Antonia, *hija de Eraclio* .... Antonio
Sabina, *criada de Antª* .... Martin
Patricio .... P⁰ de Bonilla
Un encantador .... Diego Lopez
Satan .... Juan Martinez
Otro demonio .... Diego Lopez
Emerencio, *biejo* .... Diego Lopez
Leonicio, *criado* .... Juan Martinez
Fulbino, *criado* .... Domingo Hernandez
Telemarco .... Francisco Rodriguez
Decio, *criado* .... Luis
Un hebreo .... Dominguez

El Castigo sin Venganza (1631)

Lope de Vega. Autog. MS. dated at Madrid, August 1, 1631, in the Ticknor Library, Boston. See my article, "Ueber Lope de Vega's *El Castigo sin Venganza,*" in *Zeitschrift für Rom. Phil.,* 1901, p. 411.

El Duque de Ferrara .... Autor [Manuel Vallejo]
El Conde Federico .... Arias
Albano ....
Rutilio ....
Floro ....
Luzindo ....

El Marques Gonzaga .... [Francisco de] Salas
Casandra .... Autora [Maria de Riquelme]
Aurora .... Ber[nar]da
Lucrezia .... Geronima [de Valcázar]
Batin .... [Pedro Garcia] Salinas
Cintia .... Maria de Ceballos
Febo y Ricardo ....

The Bernarda mentioned above is probably Bernarda Ramirez de Robles.

Peligrar en los Remedios (1634)

D. Francisco de Rojas Zorrilla. MS. partly autog. in Biblioteca Nacional. Paz y Melia, *Catálogo,* No. 2552. At the end, in the hand of Rojas: "Finished on Saturday, December 9, 1634, for Roque de Figueroa."

La Duquesa Violante .... la Señora Isabel [Blanco?]
Celia, *criada* .... Bernarda [Ramirez?]
Bojeton, *criado* .... [Francisco] Tribiño
Conde Federico .... [Manuel] Coca
El Almirante de Sicilia .... Paz
El Marques Alberto, *privado* .... Roque [de Figueroa]
El Rey de Napoles Sigismundo .... Francisco de la Calle
Carlos, *su hermano* .... Jacinto Varela
Infanta de Sicilia .... Maria de San Pedro
Duque Conrado .... Bargas

La Desdicha de la Voz (1639)

Calderon. Autog. MS. dated at Madrid, May 14, 1639, with licenses of June 1 and November 3, 1639. In the Biblioteca Nacional. Paz y Melia, *Catálogo,* No. 873.

Don Juan .... Pedro Manuel de Castilla
Don Pedro .... el Autor [Antonio de Rueda]
Don Diego .... [Diego de] Leon
Don Luis, *viejo* .... Jusepe [de Carrion]
Feliciano .... Pedro [Ascanio]

Luquete .... [Diego] Ossorio
Dᵃ Beatriz .... Ma. de [Heredia]

Schack, *Nachträge,* p. 87. This is the company of Antonio de
Rueda.

A un tiempo Rey y Vasallo (1642)

Comedia de Luis de Belmonte Bermúdez, del Dr. Manuel Anto-
nio de Vargas y de D. . . . MS. of the first act in the hand of
Vargas and nearly the whole third act in the hand of Belmonte.
See Paz y Melia, *Catálogo,* No. 19. The author of the second act
is probably Geronimo Cancer; v. Stiefel, in *Ztft. für Roman.
Philol., XXXII,* p. 486; Sanchez-Arjona, *Anales,* p. 295.

Rey de Sicilia .... Iñigo
Duque de Calabria .... Francisco Garcia
Almirante .... Mejia
La Infanta Beatriz .... la Sʳᵃ Maria de Jesus
Belisarda, *labradora* .... Jusepa de Salazar
Silena .... Sʳᵃ Antonia de Santiago
Laura, *dama* .... Jusepa Roman
Pasquin, *gracioso* .... Bernardo
Julio, *criado* .... Salvador
Príncipe, 7 años .... Sʳᵃ Francisca Berdugo

This is the company of Pedro de la Rosa. This play was written
for Juana de Espinosa, then (1642) the widow of Tomas Fernandez, and the manager of a company.

La belligera Española (?)

Pedro Juan de Rejaule y Toledo (who wrote under the pseudo-
nym Ricardo de Turia). MS. copy in the Palatina at Parma,
belonging to the early seventeenth century. The play was first
printed in the *Norte de la Poesia española,* at Valencia, in 1616,
a copy of which I possess. See A. Restori in *Studj di Filologia
Romanza,* fasc. 15, Roma, 1891, p. 92.

Guacolda .... la Sʳᵃ Ana Maria
Dᵃ Mencia .... la Sʳᵃ Juana [de Espinosa? or de Segura?]
D. Pedro .... Tomas Fernandez
Lantaro .... Aldana [Aldama?]

Rengo .... Simon Gutierrez
Valdiuia .... Pedro Maldonado
Laupí y Aluarado .... Villanueva
Rauco .... Lastra
Pillan y Bouadilla .... Barco
Gracolano y otro Indio moço .... Aranda

Paciencia en la Fortuna (?)

Anonymous. Copy of the first half of the seventeenth century in the Biblioteca Palatina at Parma. See Restori, *ibid.*, p. 143. The names of the actors are:

Luis de Estrada, Carlos, Juan Gonçalez, Pedro Perez, Cuebas, Nabarete, Berio, Belasco, Caçeres, Barionuebo, and Juan Mazana (added in a different hand).

Troya abrasada (1644)

Calderon. Autog. MS. in the Biblioteca Nacional, Madrid. Paz y Melia, *Catálogo*, No. 3371.

Paris .... Pedro Manuel
Hector .... Dª Veatriz
Priamo ....
Rey de Troya, *varba* .... Juan Matias
Casandra .... Maria Maçana
Elena ....Autora
Ismenia, *criada* .... Jusepa
Achiles .... Najara
Sinon .... Francisco Albarez
Menelao, *Rey de Esparta* .... Mexia
Agamemnon, *Rey de Atenas* .... Juan Antonio
Un criado de Ector ....
Viznaga .... Marin

ADDENDA ET CORRIGENDA

p. 7, n. 1.   On the *Auto Sacramental* (1520) of López de Yanguas, v. Cotarelo in *Revista de Archivos* (1902), pp. 251, ff.

p. 13.   Naharro is mentioned by Cueva in the third *Epistola* of his *Exemplar poetico*:

> "De fabula procede la comedia,
> Y en ella es la inuencion licenciosa,
> Cual vemos en Naharro y Heredia."
> (Sedano, *Parnaso Español*, VIII, p. 66.)

p. 71, n. 2.   *La Casa confusa* was represented by Pinedo's company on October 16, 1618, Baltasar Osorio and Maria Flores also taking part. (Barrera, *Catálogo*, p. 210.)

p. 122, l. 23.   Lope de Rueda concludes his *Colloquio de Camila* with the words: "Señores, perdonen, porque aqui se da fin á nuestro Colloquio," and his *Colloquio de Tymbria* with: "Señores, perdonen, que con bailar se dió fin á nuestro Colloquio." His comedia *Armelina* ends with a similar phrase, but the appeal to the audience as "El ilustre Senado," I do not remember to have seen in any dramatist before Lope de Vega.

p. 164, l. 5.   For Villahermoso read Vallehermoso.

p. 176, note, l. 2.   Strike out the words "years before," as the *Plaza universal* was published in 1615.

p. 177.   To what is here said concerning the sums received by a dramatist for a comedia we may add that in 1634 eight hundred reals was paid for a comedia by Montalvan, and nine hundred for a comedia by Francisco de Rojas and Antonio Coello. (Pérez Pastor, *Bibliografia Madrileña,* III, pp. 452, 463.)

p. 232, n.   To the playwrights mentioned may be added Antonio Coello, Antonio Solis, Geronimo de Cuellar, and Luis Velez de Guevara, who writes in 1633 that he is unable to leave his house for want of a garment to cover him.   (Pérez Pastor, *Bibliografia Madrileña,* III, p. 512.)

p. 238, n. 1.   The episode related by Hume, it may be remarked, was related by François van Aerssen, *Voyage d'Espagne,* Cologne, 1666, pp. 47–49, and repeated by Madame d'Aulnoy, who gives the Countess of Lemos as authority for her story. (*Relation du Voyage d'Espagne,* La Haye, 1693, Vol. II, p. 20.)   It is, of course, indignantly rejected by Barrera, *Catálogo,* p. 483.   It may not be amiss to add the following, concerning the comedia, also from Madame d'Aulnoy: "Autrefois, continua-t-il [D. Agustin Pacheco], les personnes vertueuses ne se pouvoient resoudre d'aller à la Comedie; on n'y voyait que des actions opposées à la modestie; on y entendoit des discours qui blessoient la liberté, les Acteurs faisoient honte aux gens de bien; on y flatoit le vice, on y condamnoit la Vertu; les combats ensanglantoient la Scene; le plus foible étoit toûjours opprimé par le plus fort, & l'usage autorisoit le crime: Mais depuis que Lopes (*sic*) de Vega a travaillé avec succez à reformer le Theâtre Espagnol, il ne s'y passe plus rien de contraire aux bonnes mœurs; & le Confident, le Valet, ou le Villageois, gardant leur simplicité naturelle, & la rendant agreable par un enjoüement naïf trouvent le secret de guerir nos Princes, & même nos Rois, de la maladie de ne point entendre les veritez où leurs défauts peuvent avoir part. C'est lui qui prescrivit des regles à ses éléves, & qui leur enseigna de faire des Comedies en trois Jornadas, qui veut dire en trois Actes. Nous avons vû depuis briller les Montalvanes, Mendozas, Rojas, Alarcones, Velez, Mira de Mescuas, Coellos, Villaizanes; mais enfin Don Pedro Calderon excella dans le serieux, & dans le comique, & il passa tous ceux qui l'avoient precedé." (*Relation du Voyage d'Espagne*, II, p. 98.)

p. 266. Among the early defenders of the comedia Andres Rey de Artieda might have been mentioned.

p. 339. In 1620 Sancho de Paz, *autor de comedias*, obtained a privilege from Cardinal Borgia to form a company of Spanish players in Naples; "and nobody else nor any other company may represent in Naples except he." (Croce, *I Teatri di Napoli*, p. 91.) In 1621 Francisco de Leon obtained a similar privilege, and in 1620 and 1621 Sancho de Paz and Francisco de Leon represented in the *Teatro dei Fiorentini*. (*Ibid.*, p. 92.) In 1630 and 1631 Francisco Malhelo and Gregorio Laredo had companies in Naples.

The Biblioteca Nacional also contains a MS. of Lope de Vega's *Quien todo lo quiere*, undated, new No. 16798. Paz y Melia, *Catálogo*, No. 2810, with the following cast:

don Ju^n .... P^o M^e [Pedro Manuel de Castilla]
don fernando .... [Antonio de] Rueda
d. p^o leon. i.e. Don Pedro .... [Diego de] Leon

fabio ....

bernal .... osorio [Diego Osorio de Velasco]

octabia .... bisenta [Vicenta ......?]

julia .... Catalina [de Acosta]

Ines .... Antª [Antonia Infante]

Dª Ana .... Jasinta [Jacinta de Herbias y Flores]

Leonarda ....

This is the company of Antonio de Rueda, about 1639–40.

The following cast of an *entremes* of the sixteenth century I owe to the kindness of Dr. Crawford. It is entitled *Entremes de un Hijo que negó á su Padre,* manuscript of two leaves in folio in the Biblioteca Nacional, in a hand of the sixteenth century.

Padre del licenciado .... Gaspar de huerta

licenciado .... Christoual de castro

muger .... michael

amo .... alº robleño

villano .... torres

There is nothing in the manuscript to indicate the date of representation. The above cast is interesting, however, from the fact that the rôle of the woman (*muger*) is played by a man (michael), which is an evidence of the early representation of this *entremes*.

INDEX

Abadia, Juan de la, 161, 162
Acacio, Juan, 52, 53, 63, 133, 221
Academia degli Intronati, 22 and n. 1
Actors and Actresses: dissoluteness
  of the latter causes women to be
  banished from the stage, 145;
  number of actors in a company,
  145, 146; actors in Molière's company, 145, n. 3; actors take several
  parts. 146; hardships of the profession, 159; Rojas's account of,
  159–160; Cervantes on, 160; actors in France, 160, n. 2; addicted
  to gambling, 164–165; account of
  his adventures related by Rojas,
  166–169; actors sometimes patched
  up plays, 171–172; they ill-treat
  the poetasters, 172–173; engaged
  at Shrovetide, 181; the salaries
  of actors, 181–188; actors from
  Madrid visit Valencia, 193–194;
  Spanish actors in Paris, 170, n.,
  339–341; character of actresses,
  206–207; women forbidden to act,
  207; forbidden on the stage in
  1613(?), 220, n. 2; when actresses
  may be visited, 246; the *Partidas*
  of Alfonso on actors, 254; without civil rights in France, 254;
  the profession of acting, 255; under the ban of the church, 256–
  257; their general bad character,
  266–267; celebrated actresses,
  268–269; temptations of, 269–
  270; Madame d'Aulnoy on, 270;
  anonymous writer on, 270, n. 2;
  visit other countries, 339–341
Admission to the theater, price of,
  112–115
Adultera (La) penitente, 198
Adulterio (El) de la Esposa, 177,
  n. 1, 307, n.
*Adversa (La) Fortuna de Rui Lo-
  pez de Ávalos*, 196
Aerssen, Francis van, 99, 319; his
  account of *autos* and comedias,
  324–328

Afectos de Odio y Amor, 198
Aguado, Andres, 40, n. 1
Aguilar, Francisco de, 83, n.
Alarcon, Juan Ruiz de, 84, n. 2,
  89, n., 93, n. 3, 94, n.; prologue to
  his Comedias, 117; 180, 186, 226,
  n. 1, 232, n., 341
Alcaraz, Diego Lopez de, 107, 109,
  n., 110, 165, 214, 215, 221–229
Alcayde (El) de si mismo, 86, 87,
  89
Alcazar, royal palace, 230; theater
  in, 230; representations in, 237
Alcina, opera, 331
Alcocer, Fr. Francisco de, 259
Alcozer, Juan de, 299
Aldea Gallega, 155
Alegria, Francisco de, 41, 204, 205
Aleman, Mateo, 154, n.
Alemana (La), dance, 74, n. 2
Alexander VI., Pope, 256, n. 2
Alfonso the Learned, his *Siete Par-
  tidas*, 4, n. 1, 252–253, 254
*Algunas Hazañas de D. Garcia
  Hurtado de Mendoza*, 180
Allen, H. Warner, 121, n. 2, 129,
  n. 2
Alleyn, Edward, 110, n. 1
Almenas (Las) de Toro, 268
Almenda, Antonio de, 68, n. 2
Almonacid, Diego de, 50, 55, 57
Almonacid, Diego de (*el mozo*), 57
Alvarez, Luis, 184
Alvarez de Vitoria, Francisco, 223
Amante (El) agradecido, 93, n. 3
Amantes (Los) de Teruel, 199
Amar como se ha de amar, 186
Amella, Juan Jeronimo, 110, n. 2,
  193 and n. 8, 223
Amor con Vista, 165, n.
Amor, Pleito y Desafio (Lope de
  Vega), 236
Amor (El) vandolero, 94, n. 1
Anaya, Maria de, 340
Andaluces, Los, 150, n.
Andreini, Virginia, 269, n. 2
Angeles, Maria le los, 63, 268

Angulo, Juan de, 183, 184, n. 1
Animal (El) de Ungria, 95, n. 4
Antonia Infante, 127, 188, 292, 294
Antonia Manuela, 155, 186
Antonozzi, Maria, engineer, 243, n.
"Apariencias," 52, 80, 97–98
"Appearances," 98, 99
Aranjuez, representations at, 238
Araucana (La), 297, n.
Arauco domado, 90
Arbeau's *Orchésographie*, 74, n. 2
Arcadia (La), 176
Archduchess Margaret, Queen of Philip IV., 211; comedias represented before, 230–231
Archer, William, 91, n. 2
Argensola, Lupercio Leonardo de, 261, 262
Arias de Peñafiel, Damian, 202, 223; greatest of actors, 267
Ariosto, his comedias represented in Spain, 21
Armona, Antonio, 36, n. 2, 111, n. 3
"Arte nuevo de hacer Comedias," 105, 287, 288
Artieda, Andres Rey de, 79, n. 1
Asalto (El) de Mastrique, 84, n. 1
Ascanio, Pedro de, 188, 190, n. 2, 194, 223, 285
Audiences in the *corrales*, 117; morality of, 120–121; in France, Germany, and Italy, 120–121; approval of, indicated by shouting *Victor!* 121–124; enter without paying, 124–126; ruffianism of, 125–130; show disapproval by hissing, etc., 279; account of Lopez Pinciano, 333–334; account of Juan de Zabaleta, 334–338
Aulnoy, Countess of, 99, 121, 239, n. 2, 270 and n. 2, 330, 331–333
Auto de San Martinho, 7, n. 1, 48, n. 1
"Autor de Comedias," meaning of, 9, 32, 33, n. 1, 169–170; dishonest practices of, 173–174; become members of other companies, 190; sums received for a performance, 194–197; guaranteed an *ayuda de costa*, 199; amount received for representing an *auto*, 200–202; *autores* between 1600 and 1603, 214; number limited to eight by the decree of 1603, 215–216; *autores* between 1603 and 1615, 216; twelve permitted by decree of 1615, 220; *autores* between 1615 and 1640, 223; appointed to represent *autos*, 300, 302; when *autos* were represented, 303–305; number of *autos* represented, 303–304; amount received for representing *autos*, 305–306

Autos, earliest, 6; represented by guilds, 7; representations in the sixteenth century, 23, 24; meaning of *auto*, 48, n. 1; *Auto de la Ungion de David*, 65, n. 1; *Auto de Santa Maria Egipciaca*, 80
Autos, *Farsas*, etc., *Coleccion de*, ed. Rouanet, 7, n. 2, 10, n. 3, 65, n. 1, 287, n. 2
Autos Sacramentales, earliest, 7, n. 1; distinguished from *autos*, 7, n. 1 and 2, 9; at Toledo in 1580, 10; represented in the *corrales* of Seville, 53; *apariencias* in, 97, 98; costumes for, 107–108; four represented annually in Madrid, 177, n. 1; *autos* written by Lope de Vega, 177, n. 1; amount paid for, 177, n. 1; sums paid for representing an *auto*, 200–202; represented before Philip III., 231; again presented after the death of Prince Baltasar, 248; opposition of the church to, 261–266, 316; the representation of *autos*, 297–312; suppressed by Charles III., 297, n.; earliest *autos* represented in Madrid, 299; *Job, Santa Catalina, La Pesca de S. Pedro, La Vendimia Celestial, El Rey Baltasar*, 299; description of the *autos Job* and *Sa Catalina*, 301 and n.; four represented annually in Madrid, 302; *autos* in Seville, 304, n. 2, 305; amount paid for representing, 305–306; sums received by dramatists for writing, 306–307; the painting of the *carros*, 308 and n.; number of *carros*, 309–310; stage for *autos*, 310–311; the properties, 311; disorder in representing *autos*, 313; edict of the Bishop of Badajoz, 314–315; the Corpus procession in Seville, 315; suppressed in 1765, 316; *autos* in the *corrales*, 317–318; great expense of *autos*, 319; sums paid to Calderon for *autos*, 321; contemporary accounts of the representation of *autos*, 325 ff.; account of Madame d'Aulnoy, 332

Avendaño, Cristobal de, 139, n. 1, 193, 199, 223, 229, 234, 235, 301, n., 305
Avendaño, Francisco de, 19
"Aventuras del Bachiller Trapaza," 173, n.
Averiguador, El, 112, n., 237, n. 1; 249, n. 2
Avila, Diego de, 13, n. 3
Avila, Juan de, 41
Avisos and Anales, 273
Avisos de Pellicer, 240, n. 4
¡Ay Verdades! que en Amor, 98
Ayala, Dª Elvira de, 49, 50, n. 1
Ayala, D. Gaytan de, 102
Ayamonte, Marquis of, 51, 53
Ayuso, Miguel de, 147

Badajoz, Bishop of, 314–315
Balbin, Domingo, 186, 200, 216, 231, 309, 317
Baltasar, Prince, 240; death of, 247; 248
Baltasara (La), 278, n. 2
Bances Candamo, Francisco de, 266, n. 1, 276, n. 2
Bandos (Los) de Verona, 240, n. 4
Bapst, G., 65, n. 1, 101, 105, 106, 137, 138, 140
"Baptism of St. John," auto, 23
Barbieri, Nicolo (Beltrame), 140
Barcelona, festival of Corpus at, 4; escarraman at, 73
Bargagli, Scipione, 22, n. 1
"Barquillos," 278
Barrera, D. Cayetano A. de la, 32, n. 3, 79, n. 1, 235, 244, n. 3, 245, n. 2, 288, n. 1
Barrio, Cristobal de, 150, n.
Barrionuevo, D. Jeronimo de, Avisos, 243, n., 244, n. 2
Baschet, Armand, 29, n. 1, 142, n. 2
Bassompierre, Le Maréchal de, 340, n. 3
Bastidor = wing of stage scenery, 92, n. 3, 97 and n.
Basto, Conde del, 180
Basurto, Diego Lopez, 184
Bayles, 69; distinguished from Danzas, 69, n. 3; the Zarabanda, 70–71; various bayles, the Chacona, Escarraman, etc., 72–73; bayles antiguos, 74; Bayle del Caballero de Olmedo, 70, n. 3; Bayle de Jácara, 125, n. 4; Bayle de la Entrada de la Comedia, 126, n.
Bella (La) Aurora, 93, n. 3

Belligera (La) Española, 83, n.
Belmonte, Luis de, 180
Benzon, Luisa, 183
Berenger de Palaciolo, 4
Bernardo de Bovadilla, Luis, 223
Bertaut, François, 118, n. 3, 121 and n., 328, 329
Bezon, Juan de, 186
Bezona, La = Ana Maria, 186
Bibbiena, Cardinal, La Calandra, 256
Blason (El) de los Chaves, 278, n.
Bocangel, D. Gabriel de, 232, n.
Bodas (Las) del Alma con el Amor divino, 211
Bonilla y San Martin, A., 16, n. 1, 71, n. 1
Booksellers, dishonesty of, 174
Borja, Vicenta de, 107
Bosberg, Sarah v., 140
Bourland, C. B., 18, n. 1
Boxiganga, the, 153
Boy Bishop (Obispillo), 127
Braones, Alonso Martin de, 290, n., 295, n. 2
Bravo, Pedro, 149
Buen Retiro, the, 238–239; representations in, 239–243; visited by the public, 240
Bulletin Hispanique, 10, n. 4, 28, n. 2, 30, n. 2, 31, n. 2, 32, n. 1, 33, n. 5, 34, n. 1 and 2, 35, n. 1 and 2, 36, n. 2, 37, n. 2, 44, n. 2, 80, n., 107, n., 110, n. 2, 141, n. 4, 163, n. 3, 165, n., 177, n. 1, 202, n. 7, 203, n. 1, 204, n. 1, 215, n. 1, 231, n. 1, 233, n. 2, 298, n. 3, 309, n. 2 and 3
"Bululu," the, 151
Burbadge, James, 34, n. 5
Burgalesa (La) de Lerma, 91, n. 1
Burgos, Antonio de, 68, n. 2
Burgos, Jeronima de, 194, 234, 258, 268
Burlador (El) de Sevilla, 90, 91
Burladora (La) burlada, 83, n., 84, n. 1 and 2, 94, n.
Burlas (Las) de Pedro de Urdemalas, 236
Burnyng Knight, the, 77

Caballero (El) del Fenix, 177, n., 307, n.
Caballero (El) del Sol, 102
Caballeros (Los) nuevos, 190
Cabello, Ana, 185
Cabranes, Diego de, 259
Cabrera de Cordoba, Luis, 111, 210,

n. 2, 211, n. 2, 214, n., 230 and n. 1, 232, n. 2

Caida (La) de Faeton, 235

Calderon, Maria, 163–164 and n., 186, 189, 269

Calderon, D. Pedro, ix, 74, n. 2, 86, 87, 89, 90, 92, 118; *El galan fantasma*, 118, n. 4; 174, n. 2, 177, n., 197, 198, 199, 202, 226, n. 1, 232, n.; *Circe*, 241; *La Purpura de la Rosa*, 241; *El mayor Encanto Amor*, 242; *Los tres mayores Prodigios*, 242, 243, n., 244, n. 2; writes the *autos* in 1645, 247; the *autos* of 1648, 248, 276, n. 2, 279; writes *saynetes*, 294–295; *autos*, 311; *autos* written for various festivals, 320; sums received for them, 321; writes *autos* till 1681, 321, 341

Callar hasta la Ocasion, 32, n. 3

Calle, Francisco de la, 295, n. 3

Camacho, Alonzo Gonzalez, 64, n. 1, 187

"Cambaleo," the, 152

Cancionero Classense, 70

Candado, Luis, 125

Candau, Maria, 65, 193, 271, n.

Cañete, Manuel, 3, n., 7, n. 1, 15, 16, n. 1, 19, n. 3, 23, n. 3

Capellan (El) de la Virgen, 93, n. 1

Caramuel, J., on the comedia, 33, n. 1; on scenery, 86, n. 1, 163, n. 3; on actors, 267 and n., 268, n. 3, 269 and n. 2, 279, n. 1; on *entremeses*, 288, n. 2

Carlos V. en Francia, 278, n.

Caro, Rodrigo, 60

Carrillo, José, xiii

Cartwright, *The Royal Slave*, 99

Carvallo, Luis Alfonso de, 280, n., 286, n. 3

Casa con dos Puertas mala es de guardar, 199

Casa (La) confusa, 71, n. 4

Casamiento (El) en la Muerte, 96, n.

Casamientos (Los) de Joseph, 177, n., 307, n.

Casarse por defendor, 65

"Casas del Tesoro," theater in, 111

Cascales, Francisco de, 227

Castigar por defender, 177

Castigo (El) en la Vanagloria, 195

Castigo (El) sin Venganza, 163, n. 3

Castillo, Alonso del, 170–171

Castillo Solórzano, A. de, 173, n. 1

"Castradores," 120, n.

Castro, Beatriz de, 147, n.

Castro, Francisco de, 185

Castro, D. Guillen de, 84, n. 1, 119, n. 1, 177, 180, 226, n. 1, 341

Castro, Luis de, 150, n., 195, 214

Castro, D. Pedro de, Archbishop of Granada, 207, 211

Catalan, Juan, 63, 184, 223

Catherine, Princess, Duchess of Savoy, 207

Cauallero (El) de Olmedo, dance, 70, n. 3

Cautela contra Cautela, 235

Cauteloso (Lo) de un Guante, 178

"Cazuela," the, 119, 128, 129, 130, 332, 337–338

Cebrian, Pedro, 194, 221

Celestina, tr. by Mabbe, 121, n. 2, 129, n. 2

Celos (Los) en el Caballo, 234, 236

Celos engendran Amor, 236

Centino, Alonso de, 12

Cerco (El) de Cordoba, 195

Cerezo de Guevara, Pedro, 147, 223

Cervantes, Miguel de, *La Galatea*, 13; his account of Lope de Rueda, 16–18; his plays *Los Tratos de Argel*, *La Destruycion de Numancia*, *La Batalla naual*, 18, 20; his *Numancia*, 21; *El Retablo de las Maravillas*, 34, n. 1; *Don Quixote*, 45, n. 2, 62 and n., 75, n. 3, 98, 295, n. 3, 312–313; on dancing, 66; *La gran Sultana*, 66, 84, n. 3, 106, n.; *La Cueva de Salamanca*, 70, n. 3; *La ilustre Fregona*, 72, n.; *El rufian Biudo*, 68, n. 3, 72, n., 74; *El gallardo Español*, 81, n. 1, 92; *La Casa de los Zelos*, ibid.; on curtains in the theaters, 84; *El Rufian dichoso*, 94, 146; *Pedro de Urdemalas*, 95, n. 1, 160, n. 1; *Viage del Parnaso*, 116, n. 5; 159, *El Licenciado vidriera*, 160; the *Colloquio de los Perros*, 172–173; *entremeses*, 289, n., 290, n.

Chacona, the, 72, 73

Chambers, "The Medieval Stage," 127, n.

Chapman, J., 179, n.

Charles V., 23. See also under *Pragmatica*

Chavarria, Andres de, 149

Chorley, J. R., 230, n.

Churchmen oppose the theater, 207 ff., 255–261

Cirot, G., 263, n. 1

Cisneros, Alonso de, 28, n. 2, 32 and n. 3, 34, 35, 43, 82, n., 131, 142,

154, n., 165, 193, 200, 202, 203, n. 1, 211, n. 3

Cisneros, Juana de, 60

Claramonte, Andres de, 54, 81, 147–149, 170, 174, 216, 221

Clavijo y Fajardo, D. José, 106

Clemencin, Diego, editor of Cervantes, 63, n. 1, 68, n. 2, 75, n. 2, 80, n., 98, 184, n., 243, n., 272, n.

Cobaleda, Pedro de, 223

"Cobradores," 64, n. 4

Coello, Antonio, 91, n. 1, 232

"Cofradia (La) de la sagrada Pasion," 26 ff., 40

"Cofradia (La) de nuestra Señora de la Soledad y Niños expositos," 27 ff.; they erect their own theaters in the Calle de la Cruz in 1579 and in the Calle del Príncipe in 1582, 33; they buy a site in the Calle del Príncipe, 35, 36; build a corral, description of, 39–41

Coleman, Mrs. 139

Collaboration of dramatists, 180

Collier, J. Payne, 27, n. 1, 28, n. 1, 34, n. 5, 37, 39, n. 1, 43, n. 1, 44, n. 3, 70, n. 1, 99, 110, n. 1, 132, n. 2, 255

Colloquio de los Perros, 172–173

Colloquio de Timbria, Colloquio de Camila, 281

Comedia del Molino, 91, n. 1

Comedias, the term comedia defined, 274–275; the various kinds of comedias, 275–277; the staging of, 76–103; Rojas, "Loa de la Comedia," 78–81; comedias de santos, 80, 144, 275; comedias de capa y espada, or comedias de ingenio, 85, 275–276; comedias de teatro (de ruido or de cuerpo), 80, 86, 88, 275, 276; comedias de apariencias, 109; comedias a noticia, comedias a fantasia, 275; the price of a comedia, 177–178; sums paid for performing a comedia, 194–197; comedias canceled by order of the King, 198, 243; opposition to the comedia, 207 ff.; no artisans permitted to visit the comedia on work-days, 215, n.; decrees regulating comedias, 208 ff.; decree of 1598, 209–210; decree of 1600, 211–213; decree of 1603, 215–216; decree of 1608, 216–220; decree of 1615, 220–223; the comedia no longer flourishing, 224; other measures enacted concerning comedias, 225, n.; comedias seldom acted in some cities, 227; comedias represented before the King and Queen, 230–246; death of Prince Baltasar, the question of again permitting comedias raised, 247; conditions recommended, 247; comedias again allowed to be represented, 248; the petition of 1646–47 to reopen the corrales, 248–249; comedias resumed in the King's palace, 249; to the public, 250; comedias written by a tailor of Toledo, 276, n.; the representation of a comedia, 277–279; gratuitous representations, ibid.; the licensing of comedias, 277; new comedias, 278, n. 1; the Loa, 279–286; the first act followed by an entremes, 286; Lope de Vega on, 287–288; contemporary accounts of the representation of comedias, 322 ff.; decline of the comedia, 341

Comedias escogidas, Vol. I, 279, Vol. XII, 88, n., Vol. XXIX, 181

Comédie Française, 101

Comella, his Cristobal Colon, 97

Comendadores (Los) de Cordoba, 92, 132, 156

"Commedia (La) dell' arte," 29, n. 1, 30, 44, 45

Como se engañan los Ojos, 234, 237

Companies of players, 145; number in a company, 145; the company of Molière in 1658, 145, n. 3; licensed in Spain, 146; compañias reales or de título, compañias de la legua, 146, 225; compañias de parte, 146–149; various smaller companies as described by Rojas, 150–154; the compañia, 153–154; the traveling of companies, 154–158; companies on the decline, 197–198; number of companies in Spain, 225. See also under Decrees

"Compañia (La) española," 149, n. 3, 195

Conde (El) Alarcos, 195

Conde (El) de Sex, 91, n. 1

Conde (El) loco, of Morales, 79, n. 1

Conde (El) Lucanor, 244, n.

Condesa (La) Matilda, 196

"Confidenti, I," 45, 46

"Confidentos italianos, Los," 142 and n. 2

"Conformes, Los," 129, n., 149, 196

Confusion (La) de un Jardin, 123, n.

Conquista (La) de Oran, 330, n.

Conquista (La) de Toledo, 180

Constancia (La) de Arcelina, 49

"Contra los Juegos públicos," 71, n. 4, 293, 294, 298, n.

Contreras, D. Antonio de, 245

Coquette (La) ou le Favori, 65, n. 1

Cordoba, theater in, 192

Cordoba, Fray Gaspar de, 211, 212, n. 1, 213

Cordoba, Maria de (*Amarilis*), 185, 186, 189, 268 and n. 3, 271, n.

Corneille, *Examen de Mélite,* 100; *Nicomède,* 145, n. 3

Corpus Christi, festival of, instituted in 1264, 4; early celebrations at Seville, 4; in 1538, 21; in 1563, 23; in 1570, 23–24, 48, n. 1; dances at, 71–75

*Corrales:—*The *corrales* of Madrid: the *corral* in the Calle del Sol, the *Corral* of Isabel Pacheco, the *Corral* of Burguillos, 27, 28; the *Corral de Puente,* 28, n. 2, 30–33, n. 4 and 5, 34; representations in, as late as 1584, 34, 43, 111; the *Corral de la Pacheca,* 28, n. 2, 29; description of, 29–30, 31–33 and n. 4; the favorite playhouse, 35; the *Corral del Príncipe,* 30, 32, n. 3; building of, 36, 39–41, 42, n. 1, 43, 44, 111; the *Corral de la Cruz,* 30, n. 2; building of, in 1579, 33 ff.; first representation in, 33; Ganassa appears in, 35, 41, 43; the *Cruz* and *Príncipe* the only *corrales* after 1587, 43, 111; changes in 1631, 112, n.; the *Corral de Valdivieso,* 31; representations in the *corrales,* when, 33; representations suspended in 1581, 35; description of the *corrales,* 41–43; closed on account of the death of Philip III., 54, 229; music in, 62 ff.; performances in, when, 111, 112; the price of seats, 113–115; two fees paid, 116; audiences in, 117; women visit the *corrales,* 118–120; men enter without paying, 124; ruffianism in, 125–129; deadheads, 126; closed during the summer, 133; the rental of, 204; the *corrales* reopened in 1621, 229; seats in the *corrales,* 134–136; closed on account of the death of Queen Isabel, 246; on account of the death of Prince Baltasar, 247; of Philip IV., 250; on account of the pest in 1682, 251; the *corrales* of Seville: the *Corral de D. Juan,* 29, n. 1, 47, 48, 113, 131; the *Corral de San Pablo,* 47, n. 2; the *Coliseo del Duque de Medina Sidonia,* 47, n. 2; the *Corral de las Atarazanas,* 47, 48, 49, 50; the *Corral de la Alcoba,* 47, 48, 50; rent of, in 1585, 205; *San Pedro,* 47, 51; the *Huerta de Dª Elvira,* 47, 49, 52; rental of, 53, 54; torn down, 59, 117, 125; the *Coliseo,* 48, 50; construction of, 51–52; rental of, 53; destroyed by fire, 54; rebuilt, 54, 59; statistics concerning, 55–57; again destroyed by fire, 60; rebuilt, 61; *La Monteria,* 48, 57–59; cost of, 59; rental of, 59, 60; destroyed by fire, 61, 65, 97, n. 2, 125, 126, 128; the price of admission to the *corrales,* 115–116 and n. 5, 117, n.; men enter without paying, 124–126; ruffianism, 128 and n., 129; plays viewed from the housetops, 130; *corrales* closed during summer, 133; visited by players from Madrid, 192; the number of representations in the *Dª Elvira* and the *Coliseo* from 1611 to 1614, 203; rent of the *Coliseo* in 1611, 205; the *corrales* closed in 1646, 248; representations again begun in the *Coliseo* in 1648, 248. *Corrales* in the Spanish colonies, 129, n.

Correa, actor, 19

Cortes (Las) de la Muerte, 312–313

Cortés, N. A., 10, n. 1, 11, 61, n. 2

"Cortesi, I," 44, n. 1

Cortinas, Dª Leonor, mother of Cervantes, 34

Costanza, La, 32, n. 3

Coster, A., 49, n. 3

Costumes on the Spanish stage, 104–105, 106; on the French stage, 105; anachronisms in plays, 105; costume an indication of rank, 105, n. 2; magnificence of costumes, 106–107; great expense of, 107, n. 3, 108; pawning of, 110

Cotarelo y Mori, E., 10, n. 1, 11, 13, 14, n. 1, 16, n. 1, 71, n. 3, 73, 85,

n. 1, 106, 112, n. 1, 115, n. 1, 143, 163, n. 3, 193, 212, n. 1, 213, n., 214, n., 216, n., 220, n. 1, 223, n., 226, n., 227, n., 256, n. 1, 251, n., 255, 256, 257–262, 290, n. 1, 295, n. 3, 316
Council of Aranda, the, 253
Court performances, when, 111, n. 2, 230–246
Crawford, J. P. W., 23, n. 3, 290, n. 1
Creizenach, W., 21, 22, n., 115, n., 138, n. 2, 161, n., 277, n. 1
Crespi de Borja, 227
Croce, B., 33, n. 2
"Cronica de los hechos del Condestable Miguel Lucas de Iranzo," 141
Cruz, Fray Jeronimo de la, 264
Cruz, Ramon de la, 295
Cruzada Villaamil, Sr., 237
Cuebas, Francisco de las, 23, n. 3
Cueua (La) de Salamanca (Cervantes), 70, n. 3
Cueva (La) de Salamanca (Alarcon), 93, n. 3
Cueva, Juan de la, 13, 49
Cumplir con su Obligacion, 122
Cunningham, F., 76

Dama (La) boba, 176, 268
Dama (La) Corregidor, 197
Dancers, Spanish, famous among the Romans, 66 and n. 2; dances at Corpus, 67–69
Dances, 71–75. See also under Bayles
D'Ancona, Alessandro, 22, 44, n. 3 and 4, 45, 46, n. 1, 140, n. 3, 142, n. 2, 256, n. 2
"Danza de cascabel," 68 and n. 2
"Danza de espadas," 69, n. 2
Danza de la Muerte by Pedraza, 6, 7, n. 1
"Danzas habladas," 75
Dar la Vida por su Dama, 232
Davenant's Siege of Rhodes, 139, 178
De Cosario a Cosario, 91, n. 1
"De Spectaculis," 262, 263, n.
Decrees regulating the theaters, 207; rescript of 1598, 207–210; decree of 1600, 211–213; decree of 1603, 215–216; decree of 1608, 216–220; decree of 1615, 220–223; other measures enacted respecting the theaters, 225; decree of 1615 a dead letter, 245; decree of 1641, 245; decree of 1646–47,

249 and n.; decree of 1653, 250 and n. 4; decree of 1665, 251
Degollado, El, 49
"Degollado," the, a fashion, 272, n. 2
Dekker, Thomas, 64, n. 4, 178 and n. 3
Delpino's Spanish Dictionary, 67, n. 3, 75, n. 3
Desden (El) con el Desden, 123
Desdichado (El) en fingir, 84, n. 2
Despois, E., 66, n.
Despreciada (La) Querida, 234, 236
"Dia (El) de Fiesta por la Tarde," 334–338
Diablo (El) mudo, 202
"Dialogos de la Agricultura," 260
"Dialogos de las Comedias," 263
Diaz, Alonso, 79, 80
Diaz, Pedro, 79, 80
"Diccionario de Autoridades," 73, n., 291, n. 4
Diez, Gaspar, 12
Dios hace Reyes, 229
Docteur (Le) amoureux, 145, n. 3
Doctor (El) Carlino, 124
Don Sancho el Malo, 236
Doña Ana, Queen, death of, 35
Doña Beatriz de Silva, 85, n. 1
Doors at back of stage, 85, n. 2, and see under Staging
Dos Amantes (Los) del Cielo, 90
Dramatists, difficulties of, with actors, 173–174; with booksellers, 174; with literary pirates, 175–176; honorarium received by them, 177–178; by English dramatists, 178–180; collaboration of, 180; morality of plays, 266, n. 2; sums received for an auto, 306–307
Drayton, Michael, 178, n. 3
Dressing-room. See Vestuario
Dueño (El) de las Estrellas, 89, n.

Eliche, Marquis of, 198, 243, n.
Elizabethan Age, number of plays, ix; morality of plays, 120
Embustes (Los) de Fabia, 87 and n. 1
Encanto (El) sin Encanto, 92 and n. 3
Encantos (Los) de Merlin, 79, n. 1
Enciso, Bartolomé de, 307
Enciso, Diego Ximenez de, 276, n. 2
English actors in Germany, 114, n.; trial performances, 277, n. 1
English court plays, 76–78

English theaters, actors, etc. See under *London*
Enredos (Los) de Benetillo, 132
Entremes de los Pareceres, 119, n. 2
Entremeses, 69; definition of, 286; *entremesos* in Valencia, 287; their origin, 287; *entremes de las Esteras*, 287, n. 2; *entremes* de Sebastian de Horozco, 287, n. 2; the *entremeses* in Lope's *Fiestas del Santissimo Sacramento*, 288; in his *Comedias*, 288, n. 4; *entremeses cantados*, 290; number of *entremeses* to a comedia, 290 and n.
Enzina, Juan de la, 3, n., 13, n. 3, 256, n. 2
Escamilla, Manuela de, 198
Escamilla, Maria de, 198
Escarraman, the, 72, 73
Esclavo (El) del Demonio, 61
Escobedo, Juan de, 204
Escolastica (La) zelosa, 91, n. 1
"Escotado," a fashion, 247, n. 2
Escuelas (Las) de Athenas, 170–171
"España Sagrada," 127, n.
Española (La) de Florencia, 88 and n.
Espeyronnière, Antoine de l', 138, n. 2, 161, n.
Espinel, Vicente, 176, n. 1
Espinosa, Ana de, 127, 164
Espinosa, Cardinal, 26
Espinosa, Gabriel de, 223
Espinosa, Juan Bautista, 223
Espinosa, Juana de, 249, n. 2
Esquilache, Prince of, 240
Esquivel, Juan de, 68, n. 2
Estebanez, Alonso and Juan, 204
Estoile, Pierre de l', *Mémoires*, 340, n. 1
Examen (El) de Maridos, 94, n. 1

Fâcheux (Les), 65, n. 1
Fairet or Ferré, Marie, 138 and n., 161, n.
Fajardo, Ana, 187
"Farandula," the, 153
Farsas sacramentales, 8, n.
Favor (El) agradecido, 94, n. 1
Fé (La) pagada, 73, 83, n., 125, n.
Fé (La) rompida, 91, n., 92
Febvre, Mathieu le, called Laporte, 139
Fernandez, Lucas, 13, n. 3
Fernandez de Cabredo, Tomas, 184, 185, 187, 196, 201, 216, 221, 242, 272, 285, 317

Fernandez de Guardo, Alonso, 185
Fernandez Guerra, Luis, 81, 111, n. 3, 227, n., 229, n. 1
Ferrer, Padre Juan, on the *Chacona*, 73
Festivals given by Philip IV., 233–246
Fête (La) de l'Amour et de Bacchus, 241, n. 1
"Fiesta de los Carros," 9, 298
"Fiestas del Santissimo Sacramento," 288, 289, n., 290, n.
Figueroa, Roque de, 118, 120; account of, 163, 172 and n., 186, 190, 200, n., 223, 250, 286, 301, n.
Fingida (La) Arcadia, 84, n. 2
Fingir y Amar, 123, n.
Fischmann, H., 66, n., 146, n.
Fitzmaurice-Kelly, J., 7 and n. 1, 14, 48, n. 1, 98, 141
Flaminia, Italian actress, 140
Fleay, E. G., 27, n. 1, 34, n. 5, 144, n. 2, 255, n. 2
Fletcher, John, 38
Floridor, Josias, 139, n. 1
Fontana, Julio Cesare, 238 and n. 1
Foulché-Delbosc, R., 328, n.
Francesquina, La (Silvia Roncagli), 46
Francisca Maria, 147
French players in London, 139, n. 1
French theater, the stage setting, 99–101; women on the stage, 138, 139 and n.; actors, 160, n. 2, 254
Fuensanta (La) de Cordoba, 190
Fuente, Tomas de la, 141
Fuerça (La) del Interes, 83, n.
Fuerzas (Las) de Sanson, 308
Furness, Horace Howard, 74, n. 2

Galan (El) de La Membrilla, 176
Galan (El) Fantasma, 118, n. 4
"Gallarda, La," a dance, 74, n. 2
Gallardo (El) Español, 92
Gallardo, Bartolomé José, 108, n., 245, n. 4, 263, n. 1
"Gallinero, El," 239, n. 2
Galvez, Isabel de, 198
Galvez, Jeronimo, 34, 35, 82, n.
Ganar Amigos, 234
Ganassa, Alberto Nazeli de, 28, n. 2, 29 and n., 30, 31, 32, 35 and n. 1, 43–44, 48, 131, 141, 204
"Gangarilla," the, 152
Garcia, Alonso, 147
Garcia, Francisco (*Pupilo*), 198, 223
Garcia de Toledo, Francisco, 150
"Garduna (La) de Sevilla," 173, n.

"Garnacha," the, 152
Garrick, David, 106
Gasque, Juan, 147
Gayangos, D. Pascual de, 16, n. 1, 68, n. 2, 111, n. 1, 231, n., 266, n. 1, 276, n. 2, 323
"Gelosi, I," Italian company headed by Ganassa, 29, n. 1
Gelves, Counts of, 49 and n.
Germany, women on the stage, 140
"Gigantones," 298
Gloria (La) de Niquea, 238 and n.
Góngora, D. Luis de, 64, n. 1
Gonzalez, Bernarda, 184, n.
Gonzalez, Gabriel, 204
Gonzalez, Jusephe, 183
Gonzalez, Matias, 204
Gonzalez, Sebastian, 149, 193, 223
Gonzalez Carpio, Dª Juana, 41, 205
Gonzalez de Salas, J. A., 69, n. 3, 98, n. 2, 120, n. 1
Gonzalez Pedroso, E., 5, n., 7, n., 311
Gradas (Las) de San Felipe, 272, n.
Graf, Arturo, 256, n. 2
Gramont, Le Maréchal de, 328, 329
"Gran Memoria," 175
Gran Sultana (La), 66, n. 2, 84, n. 3
Granada, theater in, 191, n.
Granados, Antonio, 101, n. 3, 155, 183, 190, 215, 221
Granados, Juan, 32, 34, 35, 107, n., 202
Graxales, Juan de, 185
Greg, W. W., ix, 27, n. 1, 14, n. 3, 34, n. 5, 110, n. 1, 178, n. 3, 189, n. 2, 277, n. 1
"Guardainfantes," 247
Guevara, Luisa de, 64, n. 1
Guevara, Mariana de, 184, 185
"Guzman de Alfarache," 154, n.
Guzman, Getino de, 34

Halliwell-Phillipps, J. O., 27, n. 1
Hardy, Alexandre, 99, 170
Hartzenbusch, J. E., 93, n. 3, 94, n., 134, n. 2, 180, n. 2, 228, n., 277, n. 2, 294
Haywood, Thomas, *A Woman Killed with Kindness,* 179, n.
Hazañas (Las) del Marques de Cañete, 236
Henslowe, Philip, 34, n. 5, 170
Henslowe's Diary, ix, 27, n. 1, 34, n. 5, 64, 110, n. 1, 178, n. 3, 189, n., 277, n. 1
Herbias, Jacinta de, 127, 164, 188
Herbias, Mariana de, 184

Heredia, Alonso de, 116, n. 5, 200, 216, 221, 231, 304, 309, 317
Heredia, Tomas de, 190, n. 2
Hermano (El) Francisco, 196
Hermosa (La) Alfreda, 177
"Hermosura (La) de Angelica," 233
Herrera, D. Fernando de, 49, n. 3
Herrera, Jacinto de, 180
Herrera, Maria de, 150
Herrera, Martin de, 13, n. 3
Herrera, Melchor de, 10, n. 4
Herrera, D. Rodrigo de, 42, n. 1
Herrera, D. Rodrigo de, dramatist, 177
Hija (La) del Aire, 237
Hijo (El) de Reduan, 106, n.
Hijo (El) pródigo, 10
Hinard, Damas, 87, n. 1
"Hispania Illustrata," 108, n.
History of Felix and Philomena, 77
History of Sarpedon, 77
Hom (L') enamorat y la Fembra satisfeta, x
Honorarium received by dramatists, 177–178
Honra (La) hurtada, 196
Horozco, Sebastian de, 8, n., 287, n. 2
Horses upon the stage, 79, 81
Hôtel de Bourgogne, 99, 101; women visit, 119, n. 3; rabble at, 121, n.
Hughes, Margaret, actress, 140, n.
Hume, Martin, 164, n. 1, 168, n., 238, n. 1
Hurtado de la Camara, Lorenzo, 110, 117, 223, 246, 286
Hurtado y Cisneros, D. Juan, 32, n. 3

Imperial (La) de Oton, 93, n. 3
Infante (El) de Aragon, 234
Inocente (La) Sangre, 83
"Introito," the, 281
Ir y quedarse, 225
Isabel of Bourbon, first wife of Philip IV., 237, 238, n.; her death, 246
Isabel, Princess of Portugal, 23
Italian actresses in Madrid, 142, 143
Italian comedies in Spain, 21, 22; comedy of Ariosto represented at Valladolid, *ibid.*
Italian players in Spain, 30, n. 2, 44–45; in the *Corral del Príncipe,* 143. See also under *Confidenti, Cortesi, Ganassa, Gelosi,* and *Muzio*
"Italianos (Los) nuevos," 44

Jácaras, 126, n. 2, 291–293, 298, n.
Jesus Maria, Fray José de, 262
Jimenez, Jusepe, 107
Jimenez de Valenzuela, Pedro, 195, 214
Job, auto, 200
John of Austria, Don, 164
Jones, Inigo, 99
"Jornada, 286 and n.
"Journey into Spain," 324
Jovellanos, Melchor de, xi
Judit (La) Española, 236, n.
"Juegos de Escarnios," 252
Juicio (El) final, 320
Juvenal on Spanish dancers, 66, n. 2

Labrador (El) venturoso, 234, 235
Lamarca, Luis, x–xiii, 117, n., 193, 287
Lanini, Pedro Francisco, 70, n. 3, 126, n., 290, n. 1
Lara, Salvador, 65
Laura perseguida, 278, n.
"Laurel de Apolo," 241, n.
Lazarillo, 198
Leal (El) Criado, 277
Lee, Sydney, 38, 139
Lego (El) del Carmen, 196
Lemos, Conde de, 71, n. 4, 114
Leon, musician, 63
Leon, Cristobal de, 157, 201, 223
Leon, Melchor de, 107, 214, 215
Leon Marchante, D. Manuel de, 295 and n. 3, 321
Leon Pinelo, A., 69, n. 2, 226, n. 1, 243, n.
Leoni, Leon, of Arezzo, 22
Lerma, Duke of, 101, n. 3, 102, 212, n. 1
Liar's Walk, 271, n. 2
Libertad (La) de España por Bernardo del Carpio, 49
Libertad (La) de Roma por Mucio Scévola, 49
"Licenciado (El) vidriera," 160
Licensing of comedias, 277
Limos, Juan, 141
Linares, Pedro de, 223
Lisbon visited by players from Madrid, 194
Literary pirates, 175–176
Llegar en Ocasion, 105, n. 2
Llorente, Pedro, 52, 53, 184, 216, 221, 258
Lo que puede la Traicion, 235
Lo que son Mugeres, 123, n.
Loas, 279–286; the "Loa de la Comedia" of Rojas, 78–81; va-

rious kinds of *loas,* 279; Caramuel on, 279, n.; Luys Alfonso de Carvallo on, 280, n.; Lopez Pinciano on, 280, n.; the *loas* of Lope de Vega, 281, n.; the *loas* of Agustin de Rojas, 281–284; the *loas* of Quiñones de Benavente, 284–286; the *loa de Escarraman,* 298, n.
Loaysa, Garcia de, 207, n.
Loaysa, Iñigo de, 134, and n. 2
London theaters, their foundation, 27, n. 1; contributed to the poor of the hospitals, 27, n. 1; representations in inn-yards till 1576, 28, n. 1, 30; the *Theatre,* the *Curtain,* the *Rose,* 34, n. 5; the *Globe,* 34, n. 5, 36; *Blackfriars, ibid.;* Malone on, 43, n. 1; music in, 62, n. 2, 64; gallants on the stage, 64 and n. 4, 65; Wallace on, *ibid.;* at *Blackfriars,* the *Cockpit, Salisbury Court, ibid.;* the "jig," 70, n. 1; traverses, 84; the price of admission, 114, n. 1; women visit, 119, n. 1; plays on Sunday forbidden, 132, n.; French women on the stage, 139 and n.; women appear on stage, 139–140; only two theaters in London, 144, n. 2; actors take several parts, 146; literary pirates, 176, n.; sums received by dramatists, 178–180; salaries of actors, 188 and n. 3; London visited by a Spanish company, 139, n. 1, 340
Lopez, Adrian, 237
Lopez, Francisca, 60
Lopez, Francisco, 223
Lopez, Maria, 185
Lopez, Simon, 226, n. 1, 265, n. 2
Lopez, Vicenta, 190
Lopez de Ayala, Pero, 50 and n.
Lopez de Enciso, Bartolomé(?), 240
Lopez de Sustaete, Luis, 128, 157, 202, 223, 246
Lopez de Sustaya, Jeronimo, 190, 214
Lopez de Yanguas, Hernan, 7, n. 1
Lopez Pinciano, Alonso, on the *Zarabanda,* 71, n. 1; on staging plays, 81, n. 4; on the *loa,* 280, n.; on Spanish comedias, 333–334
Lotheissen, F., 139, n. 1
Lotti, Cosme, 241 and n., 242
Louis XIV., 170, n.
Ludeña, Fernando de, 180

Lulli, Jean Baptiste, 241, n. 1
Luna, D. Alvaro de, 287 and n. 3
Luna (La) Africana, 180
Luxan, Micaela de, 268
Luxan de Sayavedra, Mateo, 154, n.

Mabbe, James, 121, n. 2, 129, n. 2
Mac-Carthy, D. F., 242, n. 1
Maccoll, N., 72, n., 160, n. 1, 173, n. 1
Machinery on the stage; see under *Staging*
Madrid as a theatrical center, x; the *corrales* of Madrid, 26–36. See also under *Corrales*
Madrid, Francisco de, 13
Maestro (El) de Danzar (Lope), 66, n. 4; de Calderon, 74, n. 2
Magdalena (La), 319
Malaguilla, Juan de, 223
Malara, Juan de, 24
Malcasados (Los) de Valencia, 119, n. 1
Malherbe, François, 340, n.
Malone, Edward, 43, n. 1, 62, n. 2, 64, 111, n. 2, 114, n. 1, 119, n. 1, 134, n. 3, 139, n. 1, 140, n., 176, n., 178, 179–180, 188, n. 3
Maluenda, Jacinto de, xii, 250, n. 2
Manganilla (La) de Melilla, 94, n.
"Mansions" on the French stage, 100
Mantzius, Karl, 45, n. 1, 137, 138, 139, n. 1, 140
Manuel de Castilla, Pedro, 187, 190, n. 2, 223
Manzanos, theatrical manager, 154, n.
Maqueda, Duke of, 239
Maravillas (Las) de Babilonia, 177
Margarita of Austria, wife of Philip III., 211; plays acted in presence of, 230–231; death of, 220, 250
Maria Manuela, 193
Maria Teresa, daughter of Philip IV., 170, n.
Mariana, wife of Lope de Rueda, 11, 12, 141
Mariana, Juan de, on the *Zarabanda,* 71, n. 4, 144; opposes the theater, 262–263, 264, n.; "Contra los Juegos públicos," 293–294, 297, n. 1
Mariana of Austria, 156, 250, 251
Marido (El) de su Hermana, 235
Marigraviela (Maria Gabriela), 63, 147
Mariscal (El) de Biron, 186

Marmol (El) de Felisardo, 84, n. 1
Marques de la Fuensanta del Valle, 233
Marquesa (La) Salucia, llamada Griselda, 18, n. 1
Marston's *Sophonisba,* 64; *Antonio and Mellida,* 146
Martí y Monsó, "Estudios," 296, n. 1
Martial on Spanish dancers, 66, n. 2
Martinazos, theatrical manager, 168
Martinelli, Angela, 45 and n. 3, 46, 143
Martinelli, Drusiano, 44 and n. 1, 45
Martinelli, Tristano, 45, n. 3
Martinez, Francisco, musician, 63
Martinez, Juan, 64, n. 1, 177; *autor de comedias,* 223
Martinez de Asensio, Pedro, 125
Martir (El) de Madrid (Mescua), 235
Martires (Los) del Japon, 134, n. 1, 195
Mas (La) constante Muger, 123, n.
Mas (El) impropio Verdugo, 123, 234
Mas (La) injusta Venganza, 123, 234
Mas merece quien mas ama, 235
Mascó, Domingo, x
Massinger, Philip, 38
Matadora (La), dance, 70, n. 3
Mayor (El) Encanto Amor, 242
Medina de las Torres, Duke of, 243, n.
Medinaceli, Duke of, 11
Mejor (El) Huesped de España, 320
Mejor (El) Maestro el Tiempo, 105, n. 2
Mejor (El) Representante, San Gines, 181
Memorial of Philip II. concerning the theaters, 208–210
"Memorilla," 175
Mendez de Carrion, D. Luis, 239
Mendoza, Fr. Alonso de, 144
Mendoza, D. Antonio de, 235, 240
Mendoza, Francisco de, 147
Menéndez y Pelayo, M., 13, n. 3, 14 and n. 1, 15, 19, n. 3, 171, n., 289, n., 297, n.
Mentidero de los Representantes, 271, n. 2
Mercader (El) Amante, 83, n. 1
Merimée, E., 293, n. 2
Mescua, Mira de, 61, 180, 186, 226, n. 1, 323, 341
Meson (El) del Alma, 310, n.

Mesonero Romanos, R. de, 239, n. 1, 272, n.
"Migaxas del Ingenio," 70, n. 3, 126, n., 272, n., 290, n. 1
Milagro (El) por los Celos, 186
Milagrosa (La) Eleccion de Pio V., 236
Milan, Dª Leonor de, 49, n. 3
Minsheu's "Spanish Dictionary," 63, n. 1, 108, n., 189, n. 1
Misterios (Los) de la Misa, 320
"Modern Language Notes," 290, n. 1
"Modern Language Review," 237, n. 1
Moeller, Frau, actress, 141
"Mogiganga (La) del Gusto," 295, n. 3
Mogigangas, 295–296
Moland, "Molière et la Comédie italienne," 46, n. 3
Molière, musicians in his troupe, 62, n. 2; *Les Fâcheux,* 65, n. 1; *La Coquette ou le Favori,* 65, n. 1; performed at tennis courts, 101; his company in 1658, 145, n. 3, 170 and n. 1; refused burial by the church, 256
Molina, Luis de, 141
Molina, Miguel de, 60
Molina, Tirso de, ix, 81, n. 1, 84, n. 2, 85, n. 1, 90, 226, n. 1, 266, n. 2, 286, n. 3, 341
Monreal, Julio, 66, n. 4, 74, n. 2, 240, n. 4, 311, n. 3
Monserrate, Diego de, 150
Montalvan, Juan Pérez de, 122, 174, n. 2, 176, n., 186, 226, n. 1, 265, n. 2, 341
Montañesa (La), 307
Montemayor, Sebastian de, 106, 142, n. 1
Montesinos, Maria de, 147
Montiel, Pedro de, 12
Monzon, Cortes de, xii
Monzon, Luis de, 149, 204
Morales, author of *El Conde loco,* 79, n. 1
Morales, Maria de, 184
Morales, Mariana de, 308
Morales, Segundo de, 223
Morales Medrano, Juan de, 108, n., account of, 162–163, 192, 196, 200, 214, 215, 221, 231, 317, 323
Morel-Fatio, A., 80, 274
Moreto, Agustin, 122, 123, 226, n. 1, 341
Morf, H., 255, n.
Morica (La) garrida, 149, 196

Morisco, his account of a play, 323
Mosqueteros, 30, 113; fee they paid, 117, 118, 119, 120; 'are the judges of plays, 121; generally paid, 126, n., 278
Motteville, Madame de, 329
Much Ado about Nothing, 74, n. 2
Mudarra, Francisco, 223
Muerte (La) de Ayax Telamon sobre las Armas de Aquiles, 49
Muerte (La) del Rey don Sancho y Reto de Zamora por D. Diego Ordoñez, 49
Muertos (Los) vivos, 173
Muestra (La) de los Carros, 290, n.
Munday, Anthony, 178, n. 3
Muñiz, Juan Bautista, 107
Muñoz, Ana, 81
Muñoz, Francisco, 116, n. 5
Music in the *corrales,* 62–64, 67, 132; music on the English stage, 64; musicians in the French theaters, 62, n. 2, 278–279
Muzio, Italian player in Spain, 21, 29, n. 1

Nabarro, Pedro, actor and playwright, 18, n. 1, 62 and n.
Naples, comedias in, 33
Nasarre, Blas, 16, n. 1
Naufragio (El) de Jonas, 308
Navalcarmelo (Naval y Abigail), 10 and n. 3
Navarro Oliver, Juan, 139, n. 1, 341
Nave (El) del Mercader, 311, n. 3
Naxera, Andres de, 195
Nichols, "Progress of James I.," 331, n.
Nicolas, Catalina de, 157
Nicomède, of Corneille, 145, n. 3
Niñez (La) de Cristo, 177, n., 307, n.
Niño (El) del Senado, 236
No Amar la mayor Fineza, 199
No hay Dicha ni Desdicha hasta la Muerte, 186
Noche (La) de San Juan, 240
"Norte de la Poesia Española," Valencia, 1616, 73, n., 83
Nunca mucho costó poco, 199
Nuñez, Esteban, 248
Nuñez, Gabriel, 132, 156, 195, 215
"Ñaque," the, 151

Obediencia (La) laureda, 93, n. 3
"Obispillo, El," 127
Obras son Amores, 53
Ocasion (La) perdida, 93, 95, n. 2
Ofender con las Finezas, 245

Olivâres, Count-Duke of, 239, 240, 243, n.
Olivares, Countess of, 239, 241
Olivares, Maria de, 186
Olivera, Casa de la (1584–1618), xii
Olivera, Teatro de la, xii, xiii; price of admission to, 117, n.; representations in, 278, n. 2
Olmedo, Alonso de, account of, 161–162, 223, 234, 292, 294
Olmedo, Jeronima de, 139, n. 1, 340
Opposition to the theater, 207 ff.
Ordish, T. F., 34, n. 5
Organos (Los), entremes, 290, n., 295, n. 2
Ormsby, John, 313
Ornero, Jeronima de, 162
Ortegon, Pedro de, 126, n. 2
Ortiz, Ana, 258
Ortiz, Francisco, actor, 183, 223
Ortiz, Francisco, author, 258
Ortiz, Santiago, 225, n. 2
Ortiz de Guzman, D. Juan, 48, n. 3
Ortiz de Villazan, Cristobal, 57, n. 1, 63, 194, 223, 233, n. 2, 258
Ortiz de Zuñiga, Anales de Sevilla, 23
Osorio, Diego, 187, 197, 202, 244, n. 2, 318
Osorio, Eugenia, 107
Osorio, Francisco, 31, 193
Osorio, Magdalena, 110
Osorio, Rodrigo, 110, 193
Ostos, Juan de, 150
Oviedo, Cosme de, 133, 151

Pacheco, D. Juan, 272
Paez de Sotomayor, Pedro, 142, 143, 258
Paniagua, Alonso de, 214
Pantoja, "Sobre Comedias," 226, n.
Parecido (El) en la Corte, 123, n.
Paris and Vienna, 76
"Particulares." See Private representations
Pastrana, Juan de, 68, n. 2
Paz, Alonso de la, 197
Paz, Gregorio de, 211 and n. 1
Paz (La) universal, auto (El Lirio y la Azucena), 202
Paz y Melia, A., 134, n. 1, 150, n. 2, 161, n., 171, n., 180, n. 3, 234–236, 250, n. 2
Pedraza, Juan de, 6, 7, n. 1
Pedraza, "Historia ecclesiastica de Granada," 191, n.
Pedro de Urdemalas, 95, n. 1
Pellicer, Casiano, 15, 21, n. 2, 26,

27, 28, 29, 30, 32, n. 3, 34, 36, n. 1, 40, 41, 42, n. 1, 43, 54, n. 3, 70, 72, n., 74, 113, 135, 137, n. 1, 143, 202, 203, n. 1, 204, 205, 212, 213, 224, 229, 240, 242, n. 1, 243, n., 246, n. 2 and 3, 247, n. 2, 248, 250, n. 1, 251, n. 1, 264, n., 291, 330, n.
Pellicer, Juan Antonio, 68, n. 3, 70, n. 3, 225 and n. 2
Peñalosa, Juan de, 199, 223
Peralta, Catalina de, 185
Pérdida (La) de España, 234
Pérdida (La) del Rey D. Sebastian, 235
Peregrino (El), auto, 311
"Peregrino (El) en su Patria," 87, 174–175, 211, n. 3
Perez, Dr. Antonio, 209, n.
Perez, Cosme, 187, 268
Perez, Fernando, 147
Pérez de Guzman, D. Alvar, 50
Pérez Pastor, Cristóbal, 10, n. 4, 28, n. 2, 30, n. 2, 31, 32, n. 1, 33, n. 5, 34, n. 1 and 2, 35, n. 1 and 2, 36, n. 2, 37, n. 2, 44, n. 2, 46, 54, n. 1, 63, n. 1, 64, n. 1, 67, 68, n. 2, 74, 75, 101, n. 3, 107, 108, 109, 110, 113, 116, n., 129, n. 2, 132, 133, n. 1, 134, n. 3, 135, 141, 142, 145, n. 2, 147–149, 150, n. 1, 155, 156, 162, 163, n. 3, 165, n., 171, 177, n., 178, 182–188, 190, 192, 193–196, 197, 198, 199, 200, 201–205, 208, 209, n., 211, n., 215, 224, 229, n. 2, 230, n., 231, 237, n., 241, n. 1, 243, n., 244, n., 245, n., 247, 248, 258, 259, 267, n., 290, n. 2, 295, 298, n. 2 and 3, 302–305, 306, 307–308, n., 309, 310, 311, 313, 317, 318, 319, 321
Performance, amount paid for, 194–197; receipts of, 202–205. See also under Representations
Peribañéz y el Comendador de Ocaña, 91, n. 1
Pernia, Pedro de, 172 and n.
Perra (La) Mora, dance, 70, n. 3, 72, n. 2, 74
Pésame (El), dance, 72, n. 2
Petition of 1646–47 to reopen the corrales, 249
Philip the Second, 33, 230
Philip the Third, fond of dancing, 66; erects a theater in the Casas del Tesoro, 111, 230; permits comedias to be represented, 211; betrothed, ibid.; autos represented

before, 231; in the Escurial, 309; death of, 54, 229

Philip the Fourth, fondness for dancing, 68, n. 2; builds a theater, 111, n. 1, 156, 164; interferes with representations at the theaters, 197–198, 243; accession to the throne, 231; patron of art and the drama, 232; appears on the stage, 232–233; neglects the greatest poets, 232, n., 237; large sums expended for entertainments, 243, n.; visits the *corrales* incognito, 244, 269, 273; death of, 250

Phillyda and Choryn, 78

"Philosophia Antigua" of Lopez Pinciano, 71, n. 1; on staging plays, 81, n. 4; on the *loa*, 280, n.; on audiences, 333–334

Pineda, Fr. Juan de, 143, n. 3, 2

Pinedo, Baltasar, 102, 107, 109, n., 131, 202, 214, 215, 304

Placida y Victoriano, 256, n. 2

Playbills. See *Posters*

Pobreza no es Vileza, 96, n.

Pobrezas (Las) de Reynaldos, 84, n. 1, 236

Poder (El) en el Discreto, 165, n.

Poderosa es la Ocasion, 234

Pope, A., couplet on Shakespeare, 39

Porres, Gaspar de, 80, 108 and n., 131, 170–171, 182, 183, 192, 193, 196, 200, 214, 215, 231, 290, n. 2, 299, 300, 301 and n., 309, 317

Posters, theatrical, 112, 133–134; in England, 134, n. 3

Poyo, Salucio or Salustio del, 174, 196, 278, n. 2, 308

Prado, Antonio de, 60, 162, 197, 223, 243, 311, 318

Prado, Sebastian de, 170, n., 249, n. 2, 340

Pragmatica de Carlos V., 19 and n., 20, 25

Premio (El) de la Hermosura, 233

Primer (El) Faxardo, 81

Príncipe (El) ignorante, 235

Príncipe (El) perfecto, 176

Private representations = *particulares*, 101; before the King, 229, 230–246; in 1622, 233–237

Propaladia, editions of, 15

Prospera Fortuna (La) de Rui Lopez de Avalos, 196

Prueba (La) de los Amigos, 90, n. 2

Pruebas (Las) de la Lealtad, 236

Psiquis y Cupido, 243, n.

Pucelle (La) d'Orleans, 101

Puente (La) de Mantible, 186, 297, n.

Puente (La) del Mundo, 297, n.

Purpura (La) de la Rosa, 241, n.

"Quarterly Review, The," 91, n. 2

Quevedo, D. Francisco de, 172, n., 278, n. 1, 240, 297, n. 1

Quien hallará Muger fuerte, 311

Quien mas miente medra mas, 240

Quien no se aventura, 235

Quinault, Philippe, 241, n.

Quinta (La) de Florencia, 83, n., 91, n. 1, 95, n. 3

Quiñones, Luis de, musician, 63, 184

Quiñones, Maria de, 187

Quiñones de Benavente, Luis, 118, n. 1 and 2, 119, n. 2, 120, 127, n., 172, n. 1, 190, 279, 284–286, 288, 289, 290, 291, 292, 298, n. 4

Quiros, Bartolome Lopez de, 192, 193

Rafaela Angela, wife of Lope de Rueda, 11, 12

Ramirez, Cristobal, 216

Ramirez, Miguel, 151, 165, 183, 214, 299

Ramos, Antonio, 216

Rasi, "I Comici Italiani," 45, n. 3, 140, n. 3, 269, n. 2

Real, the value of, 108, n.

Receipts of a theatrical performance, 202–205

Registre de La Grange, 62, n. 2, 65, n. 1, 146, n., 170, n. 1

Reina (La) D[a] Juana de Napoles, 94, n.

Reinoso, Luisa de, 147

Remirez de Arellano, Luis, 175–176

Rennert, H. A., "Life of Lope de Vega," 38, n. 1, *et passim;* "The Staging of Lope's Comedias," 40, n. 2, 84, n. 2, *et passim;* "Notes on the Chronology of the Spanish Drama," 237, n.

Representations in the *corrales*, when permitted, 130–133; *corrales* closed from Ash Wednesday till Easter, 131; no performances on Saturday, 131 (see Appendix A); always given on Sunday, 132; public representations, 132; opposition of the clergy to, 143–145; sums paid for a representation, 194–197; receipts of a representation, 202–205; gratuitous representations, 277; when representations took place, 278; account of a representation, 278 ff.; descriptions of eye-witnesses, 322 ff. See also under *Comedias*

Restori, Antonio, 70, 368

"Revista de Archivos," 108, n., 249, n. 1

"Revue Hispanique," 18, n. 1, 40, n. 2, 84, n. 2, 328, n. 2

Rey (El) Angel (El Rey Angel de Sicilia), 234

Rey (El) Bamba, 83, n., 91, n.

Reyes, Baltasara de los, 183, 279, n.

Reyes, Gàspar de los, 195, 214

Reyes, Mariana de los, 187

Reynolds, G. F., 76, n.

Ribadeneira, Pedro de, 260–261

Richter, Frau, actress, 141

Rigal, E., 100, 115, n., 119, n. 1 and 3, 121 and n., 139, 277, n. 1, 340, n.

Rios, Nicolas de los, 101, n. 3, 145, 151, 154, 215, 230, 259, 290, n. 2, 299

Riquelme, Alonso, 63; imprisoned for debt, 110, 155, 156, 172, 184, 192, 194, 200, 214, 216, 221, 231, 323

Riquelme, Jacinto, 109

Riquelme, Maria de, 163 and n. 3, 269 and n. 2

Rivas, Juan de, 32, 33

Robles, Bartolomé de, 185, 301, n.

Robles, Luisa de, 161–162

Roca Paula, actress, 141

Rodamonte Aragonés, 234

Rodriguez, Alonso, of Seville, 32, 35, 49

Rodriguez, Alonso, "El Toledano," 10, n. 4, 32

Rodriguez, Isabel, 190

Rodriguez, Fr. Manuel, 257

Rodriguez, Mariana, 150

Rodriguez, Pedro, 195, 214

Rodriguez Marin, Francisco, 71, n. 1

Rodriguez Tirado, José, 68, n. 2

Rodriguez Villa, A., 273, n. 1 and 2

Rojas, Diego de, 195, 214

Rojas, Francisco de, 122, 123, 226, n. 1, 241, n., 276, n. 2, 341

Rojas, Tomas de, 186

Rojas Villandrando, Agustin de, 3; his "Loa en Alabanza de la Comedia," 3, 13, 15, 32, n. 2, 62, 78–81, 132, n. 2, 133, n. 6, 141, n. 4, 144, 282; his life, 150; the "Viage entretenido," description of the various companies of players, 150–154; his *El natural desdichado*, 150, n. 2, 159–160, 165; anecdotes related by, 165–169, 182, 183, 189; his *Loas*, 279, 281–284

"Romancero General" (1604), 167, 294, n. 1

Romera (La) de Santiago, 236

Romero, Bartolome, 107, 155, 186, 194, 201, 223, 241, n., 291, 292, 301, n.

Romero, Mariana, 272, n.

Roncagli, Silvia ("la Francesquina"), 46, 143 and n. 2

Ropilla, 168

Rosa, Pedro de la, 107, 109, 156, 157, 170, n., 187, 194, 196, 201, 223, 242, 244, n. 2, 296, n. 1, 340

Rosario (El), of Pedro Diaz, 79, 80

Rosell, Cayetano. See *Quiñones de Benavente*

Rosenberg, M., 88, n.

Rosete, D. Pedro, 276, n. 2

Rouanet, L., 7, n. 2, 10, n. 3, 65, n. 1, 287, n. 2, 290, n., 294, n. 4, 295, n. 3, 340, n. 4

Rueda, Antonio de, 64, 65, 131, 157, 187, 188, 190, n. 2, 194, 201, 223, 285, 294

Rueda, Lope de, 3, 9–13; earliest *autor de comedias*, 9; represents in Benavente, 10; at Seville, 10; marries Mariana, a Valencian woman, 11; her suit against the Duke of Medinaceli, 11; Rafaela Anxela, wife of Rueda, and their daughter Juana Luisa, 11; his company, 12; died at Cordoba, 13; his historical importance, 14; Cervantes's account of him, 16–18, 20, 24, 25, 29, 62, 141, 170; "introitos," 281, 287, 288, n. 1

Rueda (La) de la Fortuna, 323

Ruffianism in the theaters, 125–130

Rufian (El) dichoso, 94

Rufo, Juan, 18, n. 2, 20

Ruiz, Miguel, 183

Rye, W. B., 331, n.

Saavedra, Rodrigo de, 299

Saco (El) de Roma y Muerte de Borbon, 49

Sacro (El) Parnaso, 311

Sainetes, 293–295

Saladino (El), 278, n. 2

Salazar de Mendoza, D. Pedro, 50

Salcedo, Francisco, 31, 32, 33, n. 5, 35

Salcedo, Lucia de, 184

Salcedo, Mateo de, 47, n. 2

Saldaña, Pedro de, 30, n. 2, 32, 35, 43, 49, 131

Salinas, Pedro Garcia de, 185

Salomona, Angela, Italian áctress, 46, 143

San Antonio, of Alonso Diaz, 79, 80

San Bruno, 235

San Carlos, 171, n.

San Cristobal, 128

San Hermenegildo, 23, 24

San Isidro, Labrador de Madrid, 95, n. 4

San Onofre, ó el Rey de los Desiertos, 54

San Reymundo, 190

Sancha, D. Justo de, 313, n.

Sanchez, Jeronimo, 223

Sanchez, Miguel, "El Divino," 79, n. 1, 81

Sanchez-Arjona, J., 4–9, 11, 23, 24, 29, n. 1, 32, n. 2, 47, 48–61, 63, 65, 66, 67, 68, 71, 80, 109, 115–116, 125, 126, 127, 128, 129, 130, 133, 134, n. 2, 150, n. 1, 161, 164, 165, n., 170, n., 192, 203–205, 226, n., 229, n. 3, 246, n. 5, 248 and n. 2, 293, n. 2, 295, n. 2, 304, n. 2, 305, n. 3, 306, 308, n., 309, 310, 313, 315, 321

Sanchez Baquero, Pedro, 187

Sanchez de Vargas, Hernan, 57, n., 64, n. 1, 108, 156, 157, 172, 177, 185, 186, 187, 193, 195, 196, 199, 201, 216, 221, 229, 304

Sancho Rayon, D. José, 233

Sandoval, "Historia de Carlos V.," 23, n. 1

Santa Catalina, auto, 200

Santa María Egipciaca, 197, 265, n. 2, 320

Santa Maria Magdalena, 250

Santoyo, Antonio de, 129, n. 2

Sarmiento, Pablo, 165, n.

Scenery. See *Staging*

Schack, Adolf Friedrich von, 4, n. 1, 5, n. 1, 16, n. 1, 19, 23 and n., 26, 28, 33, 41–43, 78, 81, 82, 85, 86, 88, 90, 104, 145, n. 2, 191, n., 207, n., 215, n. 2, 221, n., 226, n. 1, 228, n., 230, 233, 241, n., 243, n., 250, n. 3 and 4, 254, n. 1, 268, n., 269, n., 271, n. 2, 274, 276, 279, n. 1, 280, n. 1, 286, n. 3, 288, n. 2, 294, n. 4, 298, n. 5, 311, n. 3

Scherillo, M., 29, n. 1, 44, n. 4

Schmidt, F. W. V., 92, n. 3

Schwering, J., 339, n.

Seats in the *corrales*, 134–136

"Seguidilla," 279

Selva (La) de Amor, 236

Selva (La) sin Amor, 241 and n.

Semiramis (La) of Virués, 79, n. 1

Sepúlveda, Ricardo de, 27, n. 2, 42, n. 1, 223, n., 246, n. 1, 270, n. 1, 272, n.

Serna y Haro, Juan de la, 204

Serrana (La) de la Vera, 81

Servir con mala Estrella, 106, n.

Sessa, Duke of, 36, 172, 220

Shakespeare, 34, n. 5; *Henry V., Romeo and Juliet*, 34, n. 5, 37; compared with Lope de Vega, 36–39; *Hamlet, Venus and Adonis, Lucrece*, 37; *The Tempest*, 38; *Much Ado About Nothing*, 74, n. 2; anachronisms in his plays, 105, n.; proprietor of wardrobe at *Blackfriars*, 110, 170, 178

Siete (Los) Infantes de Lara, 49

Sigura, Juan de, 182

Simon, Manuel, 162

Sin Honra no ay Amistad, 124, n.

Sin Secreto no ay Amor, 174, n. 2

Sol (El) parado, 81

Solano, Agustin, 141, 151, 166–169, 182, 189

Solano, Francisco, 223

Solis, Antonio de, 124, 243, n.

Sommi, Leone de, 140 and n.

"Sonajas," 67, n. 3

Sotomayor, Francisco de, 190

Soulié, E., 170, n., 189, n.

Southampton, Earl of, 36

Spanish money, value of, 108, n.

Spectators on the stage, 64, 65; in *La Monteria*, 65; spectators enter without paying, 125–129; view plays from housetops, 130. For English stage, see under *London*

St. John's eve, 242, 243

Stage, the, opposed by the church, 252–266; defended by churchmen, 259–260

Staging of comedias, 76–103; no outer curtain, 82, 83; curtain at rear of stage, 84, 86; windows, balconies, walls, towers, etc., 85; doors on the stage, 85 and n.; trees represented on the stage, 85 and n.; doors at back of stage, 85, n. 2; change of scene indicated by vacant stage, 86, 87; by entering and leaving by a different door, 88; simultaneous scenery, 89; change indicated by drawing a curtain aside, 90; place of action mentioned in the dialogue, 91; vagueness of localization, 91; scene indicated by costume, 91, 92; balconies, 93; *corredor* of the theater, 93; garden and trees on the stage, 95; painted canvas, 95; importance of chronology, 96; changes in Lope's long career, 96–98; machinery and the stage carpenter, *ibid.; bastidores,* 97 and n. 2; *apariencias* and *tramoyas,* 97–99; Cervantes's remarks, 98; "appearances," 98–99; construction of the Spanish stage, 99; the stage setting of the French theater, 99–100; the stage of the mysteries, 100; Corneille objects to it, 100; complaints of d'Aubignac, 100; the stage at the Hôtel de Bourgogne, 101; poverty of scenic effects on the Spanish stage, 101–102; private representations, 102–103

Stiefel, A. L., 7, n. 1, 10, n. 1, 21, n. 2, 22, n. 1, 29, n. 1

Storie of Pompey, A., 77

Suarez de Figueroa, Cristobal, 80, 120, n. 1, 175–176, 268, 275 and n., 285

Sufrir mas por querer mas, 186, 245

Tamayo de Vargas, T., 32, n. 3

"Tamboril," the, 67, n. 3

Tapia, Juan de, 214

"Tarasca," the, 298

Tardia, Maria, 271, n.

Tejada, Juan de, 216, 220

Theater, decline of, 197; opposition to, 207 ff. See under *Comedia* and *Corrales*

Theatrical life in Spain, anecdotes concerning, 154, n.

Theatrical posters, 112, 133–134

Thomas, Hubertus, of Lüttich, 23, n. 1

Ticket scalpers, 116

Ticknor, George, 9, 14, 16, n. 1, 66, 68, n. 2, 71, n. 4, 104, 117, 118, 124, 226, 240, 241, 243, n., 252, n. 1, 226, n. 1, 269, 287, n. 3, 288, n. 1, 291, n. 2, 297, 298, n. 5

Timoneda, Juan de, 14, n., 288, n. 1

"Tonadilla," 293

Torneos (Los) de Aragon, 94, n. 1

Torre, Gabriel de la, 204, 214, 304, 317

Torres, Francisca de, 155

Torres Naharro, Bartolomé de, 3, 13, 14; his *Propaladia,* 15–16, 19, n. 3, 21, 22, 275 and n.; *introitos,* 281, 286, n. 3

Tragedia (La) por los Celos, 84, n. 1

Tragicomedia (La) de Lysandro y Roselia, 68, n. 3

"Tramoyas," 80, 97, 98

Trances de Amor, 235

Transformaciones de Amor, 244

Trato (El) de la Aldea, 190

Traveling of theatrical companies, 154–158

"Traverses" of the Elizabethan theatre, 84

Tres (Los) mayores Prodigios, 242

Turdion, the, a dance, 74, n. 2

Turia, Ricardo de (D. Pedro Juan de Rejaule y Toledo), 30, 31, n. 1, 45, n. 2; *La Fé pagada (Chacona),* 73, 83, n., 84, n. 1 and 2, 94, n., 125, n.; on comedias, 274, n.

Tutor (El), 49

Urson y Valentin, 106, n.

Vaca, Gabriel, 195, 214

Vaca, Jusepa, 268, 307

Vaca de Castro, D. Pedro, 258

Valcazar, Jeronima de, 185

Valdes, Pedro de, 52, 157, 177, 184, 194, 201, 216, 221, 229, 234, 236, 305

Valdivieso, Josef de, 311

Valencia, its importance as a dramatic center, x; origin of its theaters, x–xiii; school of dramatists, *ibid.* and 191–192; actors from Madrid visit, 193–194, 199; reopening of theaters in, 249

Valenciano, Juan Bautista, 54, 165, n., 186, 223, 229

Valenciano, Juan Jeronimo, 54, 115, 165, n.

Valiente (El) Lucidoro, 234

Vallejo, Diego de, 53, 63

Vallejo, Jeronimo, 202

Vallejo, Manuel Alvarez, 128, 133, 162, 163, 186, 199, 201, 223, 240, 245

Vargas, Andres de, 154–155

Vargas, Juan de, 149, 196
Varona (La) Castellana, 81
Vazquez, Antonio(?), 41
Vazquez, Gaspar, 32, n. 3
Vazquez, Juan (*El Pollo*), 155, 223
Vazquez, Juana, 141
Vazquez, Miguel, 141
Vazquez, Sebastiana, 147
Vega, musician, 63
Vega, Fr. Alonso de, 257
Vega, Alonso de la, *Comedias*, 15, n. 1, 170, n. 2
Vega, Alonso de la, 69
Vega, Andres de la, 109, 171, n., 177, 185, 187, 200, n., 223, 245, n. 2, 301, n.
Vega, Francisco de la, 12
Vega, Gabriel Laso de la, 294, n. 1
Vega Carpio, Lope de, ix; his residence in Valencia, x, 3, 9, 13, 16, 36, 37, 38, 39; compared with Shakespeare, *ibid.*; receives 100 ducats for his *Vellocino dorado*, 37, n. 2; *Comedias*, Part IX, 38; *Comedias*, Part XI, 38, n. 2, 40, n. 2; visits the plays of the Italians, 44, 45, 53, 63, 66, n. 4, 70, n. 3; *La Dorotea*, 74, n. 2, 174, 78, 79, n. 1, 80, 81, 82, 83, 84; *La Filomena*, 84, n. 2, 87, 90, 91, 92, 93, 94, 95, n. 2, 3, 4, 5; *Prólogo* to Part XI (1618), 96; to Part XVI (1623), 96, 97; *Prólogo* to Part XIX (1623), 98; *Epistola a Pablo Bonnet*, 98, n. 1; *Arte nuevo de hacer Comedias*, 105, 107; *Loas* to Part I, 112, n. 2; on the "vulgo," 117, 122, 146, 156; *El Castigo sin Venganza*, 163, n. 3, 165, n., 170, 172, 173; *Prólogo* to Part XVII, 174, n. 1; *El Peregrino en su Patria*, 87, 174–175, 211, n. 3; *Prólogo* to Part XIII, 175; on the stealing of his plays, 175–176; honorarium received, 177, 186; in Valencia, 191–192, 196, 199, 211; letter of October 6, 1611, 220, 226, 229, 232, n., 233; *Vega del Parnaso*, 240; *Selva sin Amor*, 241 and n.; elegy on Villayzan, 245; his comedias prohibited, 247, 260; actors praised by Lope, 267; his house in the players' quarter, 272, n., 277; his *loas*, 281, n.; never uses the term "jornada," 286, n. 3; on *entremeses*, 287; the *entremeses* in Lope's comedias,

288, n. 4; he writes the four *autos* of 1608, 307 and n., 323, 338, 339, 341
Velasco, Ana de, 106, 142, n. 1
Velasco, Francisco de, 187
Velasco Iñigo de, 134, n. 2
Velazquez, Alonso, 32, n. 2
Velazquez, Jeronimo, xii, 32, 35, 43, 71, 131, 182, 191, 193, 203, 298, n. 3, 299, 317
Velez de Guevara, Francisco, 134, 223
Velez de Guevara, Luis, ix; *Diablo cojuelo*, 71, n. 1, 272, n.; *El Caballero del Sol*, 102; writes plays for Sanchez, 172, 180, 226, n. 1, 250, n. 2, 330, n., 341
Vellocino (El) dorado, 37, n. 2
Velten, Johannes, 140
Vencedor (El) vencido en el Torneo, 236
Vengadora (La) de las Mugeres, 236
Venier, Marie, 139
Vera, Diego de, 48, 50
Vera Tassis, "Life of Calderon," 294
Verdugo, Francisca, 202
Vergara, Alonso de, 60
Vergara, Juan de, 193
Vergara, Luis de, 277
Vestuario = drèssing-room, 40 and n. 2, 92, 93
Vicente, Gil, 7, n. 1, 13, n. 3, 48, n. 1
Victor! sign of approval, 121–124
Victorias (Las) del Marques de Cañete, 235
"Vida del gran Tacaño," 172, n. 1, 278, n. 1
Vignali, Antonio, of Siena, 22
Villaizan y Garcés, D. Jeronimo de, 186, 232, 244–245
Villalba, Alonso de, 216
Villalba, Juan de, 214
Villalba, Melchor de, 214, 304, 317
Villalobos, Juan Bautista de, 54
Villalon, El Bachiller, 19, 20
Villamediana, Count of, 238 and n.
Villanueva, Juan de, 185
Villanueva, Pedro de, 194
Villaviciosa, Sebastian de, 197
Villegas, Antonio de, 32, n. 3, 150, 214, 215, 231
Villegas, Diego de, 180
Villegas, Juan Bautista de, 149, 170, 174, 186, 196, 237, 245
Villena, Marquis of, 5

Viña (La) del Señor, 311, n. 3

Virues, Cristobal de, 79, n. 1, 286, n. 3

Vitoria (La) del Marques de Santa Cruz, 96, n.

Voltaire, 65, n. 1

Wales, Prince of, visits Spain, 330, n.

Wallace, C. W., 65, n.

Ward, A. W., 37, n. 1, 70, n. 1

Wolf, Ferdinand, x, 4, n. 2, 5, n. 1, 8, n., 18, n. 2, 251, n. 1; on *entremeses,* 287, n. 2, 294, n. 1

"Woman of Babylon, The," 298

Women in Spanish theaters, 118–120; in English and French theaters, 119, n. 1, 2, 127; women on the stage, 137–143; on the French stage, 138–139; French women on the London stage, 139 and n.; women on the Italian stage, 140; in Germany, 140–141; women on the Spanish stage, 141–143; women in the ancient *entremeses,* 141; women licensed to act in Madrid in 1587, 142; forbidden to appear on the stage, 145 and n., 207; opposition to women on the stage, 212–213

Yepes, Fray Diego de, 207, n., 210

Zabaleta, Juan de, 197, 199, 290, n. 1; *El Dia de Fiesta por la Tarde,* 334–338

Zamora, casa de comedias in, 192

Zarabanda, the, 70, 71, n. 4, 143, 298, n.

Zaragoza, reopening of theaters in, 249

Zarzuela, rehearsals in, 198

"Zeitschrift für Romanische Philologie," 10, n. 1, 21, n. 2, 22, n. 1, 29, n. 1

A CATALOGUE OF SELECTED DOVER BOOKS
IN ALL FIELDS OF INTEREST

A CATALOGUE OF SELECTED DOVER BOOKS
IN ALL FIELDS OF INTEREST

WHAT IS SCIENCE?, *N. Campbell*

The role of experiment and measurement, the function of mathematics, the nature of scientific laws, the difference between laws and theories, the limitations of science, and many similarly provocative topics are treated clearly and without technicalities by an eminent scientist. "Still an excellent introduction to scientific philosophy," H. Margenau in *Physics Today*. "A first-rate primer . . . deserves a wide audience," *Scientific American*. 192pp. 5⅜ x 8.

Paperbound $1.25

THE NATURE OF LIGHT AND COLOUR IN THE OPEN AIR, *M. Minnaert*

Why are shadows sometimes blue, sometimes green, or other colors depending on the light and surroundings? What causes mirages? Why do multiple suns and moons appear in the sky? Professor Minnaert explains these unusual phenomena and hundreds of others in simple, easy-to-understand terms based on optical laws and the properties of light and color. No mathematics is required but artists, scientists, students, and everyone fascinated by these "tricks" of nature will find thousands of useful and amazing pieces of information. Hundreds of observational experiments are suggested which require no special equipment. 200 illustrations; 42 photos. xvi + 362pp. 5⅜ x 8.

Paperbound $2.00

THE STRANGE STORY OF THE QUANTUM, AN ACCOUNT FOR THE GENERAL READER OF THE GROWTH OF IDEAS UNDERLYING OUR PRESENT ATOMIC KNOWLEDGE, *B. Hoffmann*

Presents lucidly and expertly, with barest amount of mathematics, the problems and theories which led to modern quantum physics. Dr. Hoffmann begins with the closing years of the 19th century, when certain trifling discrepancies were noticed, and with illuminating analogies and examples takes you through the brilliant concepts of Planck, Einstein, Pauli, Broglie, Bohr, Schroedinger, Heisenberg, Dirac, Sommerfeld, Feynman, etc. This edition includes a new, long postscript carrying the story through 1958. "Of the books attempting an account of the history and contents of our modern atomic physics which have come to my attention, this is the best," H. Margenau, Yale University, in *American Journal of Physics*. 32 tables and line illustrations. Index. 275pp. 5⅜ x 8.

Paperbound $1.75

GREAT IDEAS OF MODERN MATHEMATICS: THEIR NATURE AND USE, *Jagjit Singh*

Reader with only high school math will understand main mathematical ideas of modern physics, astronomy, genetics, psychology, evolution, etc. better than many who use them as tools, but comprehend little of their basic structure. Author uses his wide knowledge of non-mathematical fields in brilliant exposition of differential equations, matrices, group theory, logic, statistics, problems of mathematical foundations, imaginary numbers, vectors, etc. Original publication. 2 appendixes. 2 indexes. 65 ills. 322pp. 5⅜ x 8.

Paperbound $2.00

THE MUSIC OF THE SPHERES: THE MATERIAL UNIVERSE — FROM ATOM TO QUASAR, SIMPLY EXPLAINED, *Guy Murchie*
Vast compendium of fact, modern concept and theory, observed and calculated data, historical background guides intelligent layman through the material universe. Brilliant exposition of earth's construction, explanations for moon's craters, atmospheric components of Venus and Mars (with data from recent fly-by's), sun spots, sequences of star birth and death, neighboring galaxies, contributions of Galileo, Tycho Brahe, Kepler, etc.; and (Vol. 2) construction of the atom (describing newly discovered sigma and xi subatomic particles), theories of sound, color and light, space and time, including relativity theory, quantum theory, wave theory, probability theory, work of Newton, Maxwell, Faraday, Einstein, de Broglie, etc. "Best presentation yet offered to the intelligent general reader," *Saturday Review*. Revised (1967). Index. 319 illustrations by the author. Total of xx + 644pp. 5⅜ x 8½.
Vol. 1 Paperbound $2.00, Vol. 2 Paperbound $2.00,
The set $4.00

FOUR LECTURES ON RELATIVITY AND SPACE, *Charles Proteus Steinmetz*
Lecture series, given by great mathematician and electrical engineer, generally considered one of the best popular-level expositions of special and general relativity theories and related questions. Steinmetz translates complex mathematical reasoning into language accessible to laymen through analogy, example and comparison. Among topics covered are relativity of motion, location, time; of mass; acceleration; 4-dimensional time-space; geometry of the gravitational field; curvature and bending of space; non-Euclidean geometry. Index. 40 illustrations. x + 142pp. 5⅜ x 8½.
Paperbound $1.35

HOW TO KNOW THE WILD FLOWERS, *Mrs. William Starr Dana*
Classic nature book that has introduced thousands to wonders of American wild flowers. Color-season principle of organization is easy to use, even by those with no botanical training, and the genial, refreshing discussions of history, folklore, uses of over 1,000 native and escape flowers, foliage plants are informative as well as fun to read. Over 170 full-page plates, collected from several editions, may be colored in to make permanent records of finds. Revised to conform with 1950 edition of Gray's Manual of Botany. xlii + 438pp. 5⅜ x 8½.
Paperbound $2.00

MANUAL OF THE TREES OF NORTH AMERICA, *Charles Sprague Sargent*
Still unsurpassed as most comprehensive, reliable study of North American tree characteristics, precise locations and distribution. By dean of American dendrologists. Every tree native to U.S., Canada, Alaska; 185 genera, 717 species, described in detail—leaves, flowers, fruit, winterbuds, bark, wood, growth habits, etc. plus discussion of varieties and local variants, immaturity variations. Over 100 keys, including unusual 11-page analytical key to genera, aid in identification. 783 clear illustrations of flowers, fruit, leaves. An unmatched permanent reference work for all nature lovers. Second enlarged (1926) edition. Synopsis of families. Analytical key to genera. Glossary of technical terms. Index. 783 illustrations, 1 map. Total of 982pp. 5⅜ x 8.
Vol. 1 Paperbound $2.25, Vol. 2 Paperbound $2.25,
The set $4.50

IT'S FUN TO MAKE THINGS FROM SCRAP MATERIALS,
Evelyn Glantz Hershoff

What use are empty spools, tin cans, bottle tops? What can be made from rubber bands, clothes pins, paper clips, and buttons? This book provides simply worded instructions and large diagrams showing you how to make cookie cutters, toy trucks, paper turkeys, Halloween masks, telephone sets, aprons, linoleum block- and spatter prints — in all 399 projects! Many are easy enough for young children to figure out for themselves; some challenging enough to entertain adults; all are remarkably ingenious ways to make things from materials that cost pennies or less! Formerly "Scrap Fun for Everyone." Index. 214 illustrations. 373pp. 5⅜ x 8½.   Paperbound $1.50

SYMBOLIC LOGIC and THE GAME OF LOGIC, *Lewis Carroll*

"Symbolic Logic" is not concerned with modern symbolic logic, but is instead a collection of over 380 problems posed with charm and imagination, using the syllogism and a fascinating diagrammatic method of drawing conclusions. In "The Game of Logic" Carroll's whimsical imagination devises a logical game played with 2 diagrams and counters (included) to manipulate hundreds of tricky syllogisms. The final section, "Hit or Miss" is a lagniappe of 101 additional puzzles in the delightful Carroll manner. Until this reprint edition, both of these books were rarities costing up to $15 each. Symbolic Logic: Index. xxxi + 199pp. The Game of Logic: 96pp. 2 vols. bound as one. 5⅜ x 8.
Paperbound $2.00

MATHEMATICAL PUZZLES OF SAM LOYD, PART I
selected and edited by M. Gardner

Choice puzzles by the greatest American puzzle creator and innovator. Selected from his famous collection, "Cyclopedia of Puzzles," they retain the unique style and historical flavor of the originals. There are posers based on arithmetic, algebra, probability, game theory, route tracing, topology, counter and sliding block, operations research, geometrical dissection. Includes the famous "14-15" puzzle which was a national craze, and his "Horse of a Different Color" which sold millions of copies. 117 of his most ingenious puzzles in all. 120 line drawings and diagrams. Solutions. Selected references. xx + 167pp. 5⅜ x 8.
Paperbound $1.00

STRING FIGURES AND HOW TO MAKE THEM, *Caroline Furness Jayne*

107 string figures plus variations selected from the best primitive and modern examples developed by Navajo, Apache, pygmies of Africa, Eskimo, in Europe, Australia, China, etc. The most readily understandable, easy-to-follow book in English on perennially popular recreation. Crystal-clear exposition; step-by-step diagrams. Everyone from kindergarten children to adults looking for unusual diversion will be endlessly amused. Index. Bibliography. Introduction by A. C. Haddon. 17 full-page plates, 960 illustrations. xxiii + 401pp. 5⅜ x 8½.
Paperbound $2.00

PAPER FOLDING FOR BEGINNERS, *W. D. Murray and F. J. Rigney*

A delightful introduction to the varied and entertaining Japanese art of origami (paper folding), with a full, crystal-clear text that anticipates every difficulty; over 275 clearly labeled diagrams of all important stages in creation. You get results at each stage, since complex figures are logically developed from simpler ones. 43 different pieces are explained: sailboats, frogs, roosters, etc. 6 photographic plates. 279 diagrams. 95pp. 5⅝ x 8⅜. Paperbound $1.00

PRINCIPLES OF ART HISTORY,

H. Wölfflin

Analyzing such terms as "baroque," "classic," "neoclassic," "primitive," "picturesque," and 164 different works by artists like Botticelli, van Cleve, Dürer, Hobbema, Holbein, Hals, Rembrandt, Titian, Brueghel, Vermeer, and many others, the author establishes the classifications of art history and style on a firm, concrete basis. This classic of art criticism shows what really occurred between the 14th-century primitives and the sophistication of the 18th century in terms of basic attitudes and philosophies. "A remarkable lesson in the art of seeing," *Sat. Rev. of Literature*. Translated from the 7th German edition. 150 illustrations. 254pp. 6⅛ x 9¼.   Paperbound $2.00

PRIMITIVE ART,

Franz Boas

This authoritative and exhaustive work by a great American anthropologist covers the entire gamut of primitive art. Pottery, leatherwork, metal work, stone work, wood, basketry, are treated in detail. Theories of primitive art, historical depth in art history, technical virtuosity, unconscious levels of patterning, symbolism, styles, literature, music, dance, etc. A must book for the interested layman, the anthropologist, artist, handicrafter (hundreds of unusual motifs), and the historian. Over 900 illustrations (50 ceramic vessels, 12 totem poles, etc.). 376pp. 5⅜ x 8.   Paperbound $2.25

THE GENTLEMAN AND CABINET MAKER'S DIRECTOR,

Thomas Chippendale

A reprint of the 1762 catalogue of furniture designs that went on to influence generations of English and Colonial and Early Republic American furniture makers. The 200 plates, most of them full-page sized, show Chippendale's designs for French (Louis XV), Gothic, and Chinese-manner chairs, sofas, canopy and dome beds, cornices, chamber organs, cabinets, shaving tables, commodes, picture frames, frets, candle stands, chimney pieces, decorations, etc. The drawings are all elegant and highly detailed; many include construction diagrams and elevations. A supplement of 24 photographs shows surviving pieces of original and Chippendale-style pieces of furniture. Brief biography of Chippendale by N. I. Bienenstock, editor of *Furniture World*. Reproduced from the 1762 edition. 200 plates, plus 19 photographic plates. vi + 249pp. 9⅛ x 12¼.   Paperbound $3.50

AMERICAN ANTIQUE FURNITURE: A BOOK FOR AMATEURS,

Edgar G. Miller, Jr.

Standard introduction and practical guide to identification of valuable American antique furniture. 2115 illustrations, mostly photographs taken by the author in 148 private homes, are arranged in chronological order in extensive chapters on chairs, sofas, chests, desks, bedsteads, mirrors, tables, clocks, and other articles. Focus is on furniture accessible to the collector, including simpler pieces and a larger than usual coverage of Empire style. Introductory chapters identify structural elements, characteristics of various styles, how to avoid fakes, etc. "We are frequently asked to name some book on American furniture that will meet the requirements of the novice collector, the beginning dealer, and . . . the general public. . . . We believe Mr. Miller's two volumes more completely satisfy this specification than any other work," *Antiques*. Appendix. Index. Total of vi + 1106pp. 7⅞ x 10¾.

Two volume set, paperbound $7.50

THE BAD CHILD'S BOOK OF BEASTS, MORE BEASTS FOR WORSE CHILDREN, and A MORAL ALPHABET, *H. Belloc*
Hardly and anthology of humorous verse has appeared in the last 50 years without at least a couple of these famous nonsense verses. But one must see the entire volumes — with all the delightful original illustrations by Sir Basil Blackwood — to appreciate fully Belloc's charming and witty verses that play so subacidly on the platitudes of life and morals that beset his day — and ours. A great humor classic. Three books in one. Total of 157pp. 5⅜ x 8.
Paperbound $1.00

THE DEVIL'S DICTIONARY, *Ambrose Bierce*
Sardonic and irreverent barbs puncturing the pomposities and absurdities of American politics, business, religion, literature, and arts, by the country's greatest satirist in the classic tradition. Epigrammatic as Shaw, piercing as Swift, American as Mark Twain, Will Rogers, and Fred Allen, Bierce will always remain the favorite of a small coterie of enthusiasts, and of writers and speakers whom he supplies with "some of the most gorgeous witticisms of the English language" (H. L. Mencken). Over 1000 entries in alphabetical order. 144pp. 5⅜ x 8.
Paperbound $1.00

THE COMPLETE NONSENSE OF EDWARD LEAR.
This is the only complete edition of this master of gentle madness available at a popular price. *A Book of Nonsense, Nonsense Songs, More Nonsense Songs and Stories* in their entirety with all the old favorites that have delighted children and adults for years. The Dong With A Luminous Nose, The Jumblies, The Owl and the Pussycat, and hundreds of other bits of wonderful nonsense. 214 limericks, 3 sets of Nonsense Botany, 5 Nonsense Alphabets, 546 drawings by Lear himself, and much more. 320pp. 5⅜ x 8.
Paperbound $1.00

THE WIT AND HUMOR OF OSCAR WILDE, *ed. by Alvin Redman*
Wilde at his most brilliant, in 1000 epigrams exposing weaknesses and hypocrisies of "civilized" society. Divided into 49 categories—sin, wealth, women, America, etc.—to aid writers, speakers. Includes excerpts from his trials, books, plays, criticism. Formerly "The Epigrams of Oscar Wilde." Introduction by Vyvyan Holland, Wilde's only living son. Introductory essay by editor. 260pp. 5⅜ x 8.
Paperbound $1.00

A CHILD'S PRIMER OF NATURAL HISTORY, *Oliver Herford*
Scarcely an anthology of whimsy and humor has appeared in the last 50 years without a contribution from Oliver Herford. Yet the works from which these examples are drawn have been almost impossible to obtain! Here at last are Herford's improbable definitions of a menagerie of familiar and weird animals, each verse illustrated by the author's own drawings. 24 drawings in 2 colors; 24 additional drawings. vii + 95pp. 6½ x 6.
Paperbound $1.00

THE BROWNIES: THEIR BOOK, *Palmer Cox*
The book that made the Brownies a household word. Generations of readers have enjoyed the antics, predicaments and adventures of these jovial sprites, who emerge from the forest at night to play or to come to the aid of a deserving human. Delightful illustrations by the author decorate nearly every page. 24 short verse tales with 266 illustrations. 155pp. 6⅝ x 9¼.
Paperbound $1.50

THE PRINCIPLES OF PSYCHOLOGY,
William James
The full long-course, unabridged, of one of the great classics of Western literature and science. Wonderfully lucid descriptions of human mental activity, the stream of thought, consciousness, time perception, memory, imagination, emotions, reason, abnormal phenomena, and similar topics. Original contributions are integrated with the work of such men as Berkeley, Binet, Mills, Darwin, Hume, Kant, Royce, Schopenhauer, Spinoza, Locke, Descartes, Galton, Wundt, Lotze, Herbart, Fechner, and scores of others. All contrasting interpretations of mental phenomena are examined in detail—introspective analysis, philosophical interpretation, and experimental research. "A classic," *Journal of Consulting Psychology.* "The main lines are as valid as ever," *Psychoanalytical Quarterly.* "Standard reading . . . a classic of interpretation," *Psychiatric Quarterly.* 94 illustrations. 1408pp. 5⅜ x 8.
Vol. 1 Paperbound $2.50, Vol. 2 Paperbound $2.50,
The set $5.00

VISUAL ILLUSIONS: THEIR CAUSES, CHARACTERISTICS AND APPLICATIONS,
M. Luckiesh
"Seeing is deceiving," asserts the author of this introduction to virtually every type of optical illusion known. The text both describes and explains the principles involved in color illusions, figure-ground, distance illusions, etc. 100 photographs, drawings and diagrams prove how easy it is to fool the sense: circles that aren't round, parallel lines that seem to bend, stationary figures that seem to move as you stare at them — illustration after illustration strains our credulity at what we see. Fascinating book from many points of view, from applications for artists, in camouflage, etc. to the psychology of vision. New introduction by William Ittleson, Dept. of Psychology, Queens College. Index. Bibliography. xxi + 252pp. 5⅜ x 8½. Paperbound $1.50

FADS AND FALLACIES IN THE NAME OF SCIENCE,
Martin Gardner
This is the standard account of various cults, quack systems, and delusions which have masqueraded as science: hollow earth fanatics. Reich and orgone sex energy, dianetics, Atlantis, multiple moons, Forteanism, flying saucers, medical fallacies like iridiagnosis, zone therapy, etc. A new chapter has been added on Bridey Murphy, psionics, and other recent manifestations in this field. This is a fair, reasoned appraisal of eccentric theory which provides excellent inoculation against cleverly masked nonsense. "Should be read by everyone, scientist and non-scientist alike," R. T. Birge, Prof. Emeritus of Physics, Univ. of California; Former President, American Physical Society. Index. x + 365pp. 5⅜ x 8. Paperbound $1.85

ILLUSIONS AND DELUSIONS OF THE SUPERNATURAL AND THE OCCULT,
D. H. Rawcliffe
Holds up to rational examination hundreds of persistent delusions including crystal gazing, automatic writing, table turning, mediumistic trances, mental healing, stigmata, lycanthropy, live burial, the Indian Rope Trick, spiritualism, dowsing, telepathy, clairvoyance, ghosts, ESP, etc. The author explains and exposes the mental and physical deceptions involved, making this not only an exposé of supernatural phenomena, but a valuable exposition of characteristic types of abnormal psychology. Originally titled "The Psychology of the Occult." 14 illustrations. Index. 551pp. 5⅜ x 8. Paperbound $2.25

FAIRY TALE COLLECTIONS, *edited by Andrew Lang*
Andrew Lang's fairy tale collections make up the richest shelf-full of traditional children's stories anywhere available. Lang supervised the translation of stories from all over the world—familiar European tales collected by Grimm, animal stories from Negro Africa, myths of primitive Australia, stories from Russia, Hungary, Iceland, Japan, and many other countries. Lang's selection of translations are unusually high; many authorities consider that the most familiar tales find their best versions in these volumes. All collections are richly decorated and illustrated by H. J. Ford and other artists.

THE BLUE FAIRY BOOK. 37 stories. 138 illustrations. ix + 390pp. 5⅜ x 8½.
Paperbound $1.50

THE GREEN FAIRY BOOK. 42 stories. 100 illustrations. xiii + 366pp. 5⅜ x 8½.
Paperbound $1.50

THE BROWN FAIRY BOOK. 32 stories. 50 illustrations, 8 in color. xii + 350pp. 5⅜ x 8½.
Paperbound $1.50

THE BEST TALES OF HOFFMANN, *edited by E. F. Bleiler*
10 stories by E. T. A. Hoffmann, one of the greatest of all writers of fantasy. The tales include "The Golden Flower Pot," "Automata," "A New Year's Eve Adventure," "Nutcracker and the King of Mice," "Sand-Man," and others. Vigorous characterizations of highly eccentric personalities, remarkably imaginative situations, and intensely fast pacing has made these tales popular all over the world for 150 years. Editor's introduction. 7 drawings by Hoffmann. xxxiii + 419pp. 5⅜ x 8½.
Paperbound $2.00

GHOST AND HORROR STORIES OF AMBROSE BIERCE,
edited by E. F. Bleiler
Morbid, eerie, horrifying tales of possessed poets, shabby aristocrats, revived corpses, and haunted malefactors. Widely acknowledged as the best of their kind between Poe and the moderns, reflecting their author's inner torment and bitter view of life. Includes "Damned Thing," "The Middle Toe of the Right Foot," "The Eyes of the Panther," "Visions of the Night," "Moxon's Master," and over a dozen others. Editor's introduction. xxii + 199pp. 5⅜ x 8½.
Paperbound $1.25

THREE GOTHIC NOVELS, *edited by E. F. Bleiler*
Originators of the still popular Gothic novel form, influential in ushering in early 19th-century Romanticism. Horace Walpole's *Castle of Otranto*, William Beckford's *Vathek*, John Polidori's *The Vampyre*, and a *Fragment* by Lord Byron are enjoyable as exciting reading or as documents in the history of English literature. Editor's introduction. xi + 291pp. 5⅜ x 8½.
Paperbound $2.00

BEST GHOST STORIES OF LEFANU, *edited by E. F. Bleiler*
Though admired by such critics as V. S. Pritchett, Charles Dickens and Henry James, ghost stories by the Irish novelist Joseph Sheridan LeFanu have never become as widely known as his detective fiction. About half of the 16 stories in this collection have never before been available in America. Collection includes "Carmilla" (perhaps the best vampire story ever written), "The Haunted Baronet," "The Fortunes of Sir Robert Ardagh," and the classic "Green Tea." Editor's introduction. 7 contemporary illustrations. Portrait of LeFanu. xii + 467pp. 5⅜ x 8.
Paperbound $2.00

EASY-TO-DO ENTERTAINMENTS AND DIVERSIONS WITH COINS, CARDS, STRING, PAPER AND MATCHES, *R. M. Abraham*
Over 300 tricks, games and puzzles will provide young readers with absorbing fun. Sections on card games; paper-folding; tricks with coins, matches and pieces of string; games for the agile; toy-making from common household objects; mathematical recreations; and 50 miscellaneous pastimes. Anyone in charge of groups of youngsters, including hard-pressed parents, and in need of suggestions on how to keep children sensibly amused and quietly content will find this book indispensable. Clear, simple text, copious number of delightful line drawings and illustrative diagrams. Originally titled "Winter Nights' Entertainments." Introduction by Lord Baden Powell. 329 illustrations. v + 186pp. 5⅜ x 8½.   Paperbound $1.00

AN INTRODUCTION TO CHESS MOVES AND TACTICS SIMPLY EXPLAINED, *Leonard Barden*
Beginner's introduction to the royal game. Names, possible moves of the pieces, definitions of essential terms, how games are won, etc. explained in 30-odd pages. With this background you'll be able to sit right down and play. Balance of book teaches strategy — openings, middle game, typical endgame play, and suggestions for improving your game. A sample game is fully analyzed. True middle-level introduction, teaching you all the essentials without oversimplifying or losing you in a maze of detail. 58 figures. 102pp. 5⅜ x 8½.   Paperbound $1.00

LASKER'S MANUAL OF CHESS, *Dr. Emanuel Lasker*
Probably the greatest chess player of modern times, Dr. Emanuel Lasker held the world championship 28 years, independent of passing schools or fashions. This unmatched study of the game, chiefly for intermediate to skilled players, analyzes basic methods, combinations, position play, the aesthetics of chess, dozens of different openings, etc., with constant reference to great modern games. Contains a brilliant exposition of Steinitz's important theories. Introduction by Fred Reinfeld. Tables of Lasker's tournament record. 3 indices. 308 diagrams. 1 photograph. xxx + 349pp. 5⅜ x 8.   Paperbound $2.25

COMBINATIONS: THE HEART OF CHESS, *Irving Chernev*
Step-by-step from simple combinations to complex, this book, by a well-known chess writer, shows you the intricacies of pins, counter-pins, knight forks, and smothered mates. Other chapters show alternate lines of play to those taken in actual championship games; boomerang combinations; classic examples of brilliant combination play by Nimzovich, Rubinstein, Tarrasch, Botvinnik, Alekhine and Capablanca. Index. 356 diagrams. ix + 245pp. 5⅜ x 8½.   Paperbound $1.85

HOW TO SOLVE CHESS PROBLEMS, *K. S. Howard*
Full of practical suggestions for the fan or the beginner — who knows only the moves of the chessmen. Contains preliminary section and 58 two-move, 46 three-move, and 8 four-move problems composed by 27 outstanding American problem creators in the last 30 years. Explanation of all terms and exhaustive index. "Just what is wanted for the student," Brian Harley. 112 problems, solutions. vi + 171pp. 5⅜ x 8.   Paperbound $1.35

SOCIAL THOUGHT FROM LORE TO SCIENCE,
H. E. Barnes and H. Becker
An immense survey of sociological thought and ways of viewing, studying, planning, and reforming society from earliest times to the present. Includes thought on society of preliterate peoples, ancient non-Western cultures, and every great movement in Europe, America, and modern Japan. Analyzes hundreds of great thinkers: Plato, Augustine, Bodin, Vico, Montesquieu, Herder, Comte, Marx, etc. Weighs the contributions of utopians, sophists, fascists and communists; economists, jurists, philosophers, ecclesiastics, and every 19th and 20th century school of scientific sociology, anthropology, and social psychology throughout the world. Combines topical, chronological, and regional approaches, treating the evolution of social thought as a process rather than as a series of mere topics. "Impressive accuracy, competence, and discrimination . . . easily the best single survey," *Nation*. Thoroughly revised, with new material up to 1960. 2 indexes. Over 2200 bibliographical notes. Three volume set. Total of 1586pp. 5⅜ x 8.
Vol. 1 Paperbound $2.75, Vol. 2 Paperbound $2.75, Vol. 3 Paperbound $2.50
The set $8.00

A HISTORY OF HISTORICAL WRITING, *Harry Elmer Barnes*
Virtually the only adequate survey of the whole course of historical writing in a single volume. Surveys developments from the beginnings of historiography in the ancient Near East and the Classical World, up through the Cold War. Covers major historians in detail, shows interrelationship with cultural background, makes clear individual contributions, evaluates and estimates importance; also enormously rich upon minor authors and thinkers who are usually passed over. Packed with scholarship and learning, clear, easily written. Indispensable to every student of history. Revised and enlarged up to 1961. Index and bibliography. xv + 442pp. 5⅜ x 8½.   Paperbound $2.50

JOHANN SEBASTIAN BACH, *Philipp Spitta*
The complete and unabridged text of the definitive study of Bach. Written some 70 years ago, it is still unsurpassed for its coverage of nearly all aspects of Bach's life and work. There could hardly be a finer non-technical introduction to Bach's music than the detailed, lucid analyses which Spitta provides for hundreds of individual pieces. 26 solid pages are devoted to the B minor mass, for example, and 30 pages to the glorious St. Matthew Passion. This monumental set also includes a major analysis of the music of the 18th century: Buxtehude, Pachelbel, etc. "Unchallenged as the last word on one of the supreme geniuses of music," John Barkham, *Saturday Review Syndicate*. Total of 1819pp. Heavy cloth binding. 5⅜ x 8.
Two volume set, clothbound $13.50

BEETHOVEN AND HIS NINE SYMPHONIES, *George Grove*
In this modern middle-level classic of musicology Grove not only analyzes all nine of Beethoven's symphonies very thoroughly in terms of their musical structure, but also discusses the circumstances under which they were written, Beethoven's stylistic development, and much other background material. This is an extremely rich book, yet very easily followed; it is highly recommended to anyone seriously interested in music. Over 250 musical passages. Index. viii + 407pp. 5⅜ x 8.
Paperbound $2.00

THREE SCIENCE FICTION NOVELS,
John Taine
Acknowledged by many as the best SF writer of the 1920's, Taine (under the name Eric Temple Bell) was also a Professor of Mathematics of considerable renown. Reprinted here are *The Time Stream*, generally considered Taine's best, *The Greatest Game*, a biological-fiction novel, and *The Purple Sapphire*, involving a supercivilization of the past. Taine's stories tie fantastic narratives to frameworks of original and logical scientific concepts. Speculation is often profound on such questions as the nature of time, concept of entropy, cyclical universes, etc. 4 contemporary illustrations. v + 532pp. 5⅜ x 8⅜.

Paperbound $2.00

SEVEN SCIENCE FICTION NOVELS,
H. G. Wells
Full unabridged texts of 7 science-fiction novels of the master. Ranging from biology, physics, chemistry, astronomy, to sociology and other studies, Mr. Wells extrapolates whole worlds of strange and intriguing character. "One will have to go far to match this for entertainment, excitement, and sheer pleasure . . ."*New York Times*. Contents: The Time Machine, The Island of Dr. Moreau, The First Men in the Moon, The Invisible Man, The War of the Worlds, The Food of the Gods, In The Days of the Comet. 1015pp. 5⅜ x 8.

Clothbound $5.00

28 SCIENCE FICTION STORIES OF H. G. WELLS.
Two full, unabridged novels, *Men Like Gods* and *Star Begotten*, plus 26 short stories by the master science-fiction writer of all time! Stories of space, time, invention, exploration, futuristic adventure. Partial contents: *The Country of the Blind, In the Abyss, The Crystal Egg, The Man Who Could Work Miracles, A Story of Days to Come, The Empire of the Ants, The Magic Shop, The Valley of the Spiders, A Story of the Stone Age, Under the Knife, Sea Raiders,* etc. An indispensable collection for the library of anyone interested in science fiction adventure. 928pp. 5⅜ x 8.

Clothbound $4.50

THREE MARTIAN NOVELS,
Edgar Rice Burroughs
Complete, unabridged reprinting, in one volume, of Thuvia, Maid of Mars; Chessmen of Mars; The Master Mind of Mars. Hours of science-fiction adventure by a modern master storyteller. Reset in large clear type for easy reading. 16 illustrations by J. Allen St. John. vi + 499pp. 5⅜ x 8½.

Paperbound $1.85

AN INTELLECTUAL AND CULTURAL HISTORY OF THE WESTERN WORLD,
Harry Elmer Barnes
Monumental 3-volume survey of intellectual development of Europe from primitive cultures to the present day. Every significant product of human intellect traced through history: art, literature, mathematics, physical sciences, medicine, music, technology, social sciences, religions, jurisprudence, education, etc. Presentation is lucid and specific, analyzing in detail specific discoveries, theories, literary works, and so on. Revised (1965) by recognized scholars in specialized fields under the direction of Prof. Barnes. Revised bibliography. Indexes. 24 illustrations. Total of xxix + 1318pp.
Vol. 1 Paperbound $2.00, Vol. 2 Paperbound $2.00, Vol. 3 Paperbound $2.00,

The set $6.00

HEAR ME TALKIN' TO YA, *edited by Nat Shapiro and Nat Hentoff*
In their own words, Louis Armstrong, King Oliver, Fletcher Henderson, Bunk Johnson, Bix Beiderbecke, Billy Holiday, Fats Waller, Jelly Roll Morton, Duke Ellington, and many others comment on the origins of jazz in New Orleans and its growth in Chicago's South Side, Kansas City's jam sessions, Depression Harlem, and the modernism of the West Coast schools. Taken from taped conversations, letters, magazine articles, other first-hand sources. Editors' introduction. xvi + 429pp. 5⅜ x 8½.　　　　Paperbound $2.00

THE JOURNAL OF HENRY D. THOREAU
A 25-year record by the great American observer and critic, as complete a record of a great man's inner life as is anywhere available. Thoreau's Journals served him as raw material for his formal pieces, as a place where he could develop his ideas, as an outlet for his interests in wild life and plants, in writing as an art, in classics of literature, Walt Whitman and other contemporaries, in politics, slavery, individual's relation to the State, etc. The Journals present a portrait of a remarkable man, and are an observant social history. Unabridged republication of 1906 edition, Bradford Torrey and Francis H. Allen, editors. Illustrations. Total of 1888pp. 8⅜ x 12¼.
　　　　　　　　　　　　　　　Two volume set, clothbound $25.00

A SHAKESPEARIAN GRAMMAR, *E. A. Abbott*
Basic reference to Shakespeare and his contemporaries, explaining through thousands of quotations from Shakespeare, Jonson, Beaumont and Fletcher, North's *Plutarch* and other sources the grammatical usage differing from the modern. First published in 1870 and written by a scholar who spent much of his life isolating principles of Elizabethan language, the book is unlikely ever to be superseded. Indexes. xxiv + 511pp. 5⅜ x 8½.　　　Paperbound $2.75

FOLK-LORE OF SHAKESPEARE, *T. F. Thistelton Dyer*
Classic study, drawing from Shakespeare a large body of references to supernatural beliefs, terminology of falconry and hunting, games and sports, good luck charms, marriage customs, folk medicines, superstitions about plants, animals, birds, argot of the underworld, sexual slang of London, proverbs, drinking customs, weather lore, and much else. From full compilation comes a mirror of the 17th-century popular mind. Index. ix + 526pp. 5⅜ x 8½.
　　　　　　　　　　　　　　　Paperbound $2.50

THE NEW VARIORUM SHAKESPEARE, *edited by H. H. Furness*
By far the richest editions of the plays ever produced in any country or language. Each volume contains complete text (usually First Folio) of the play, all variants in Quarto and other Folio texts, editorial changes by every major editor to Furness's own time (1900), footnotes to obscure references or language, extensive quotes from literature of Shakespearian criticism, essays on plot sources (often reprinting sources in full), and much more.

HAMLET, *edited by H. H. Furness*
Total of xxvi + 905pp. 5⅜ x 8½.　　　Two volume set, paperbound $4.75

TWELFTH NIGHT, *edited by H. H. Furness*
Index. xxii + 434pp. 5⅜ x 8½.
　　　　　　　　　　　　　　　Paperbound $2.25

La Boheme by Giacomo Puccini,
translated and introduced by Ellen H. Bleiler
Complete handbook for the operagoer, with everything needed for full enjoyment except the musical score itself. Complete Italian libretto, with new, modern English line-by-line translation—the only libretto printing all repeats; biography of Puccini; the librettists; background to the opera, Murger's La Boheme, etc.; circumstances of composition and performances; plot summary; and pictorial section of 73 illustrations showing Puccini, famous singers and performances, etc. Large clear type for easy reading. 124pp. 5⅜ x 8½.
Paperbound $1.00

Antonio Stradivari: His Life and Work (1644-1737),
W. Henry Hill, Arthur F. Hill, and Alfred E. Hill
Still the only book that really delves into life and art of the incomparable Italian craftsman, maker of the finest musical instruments in the world today. The authors, expert violin-makers themselves, discuss Stradivari's ancestry, his construction and finishing techniques, distinguished characteristics of many of his instruments and their locations. Included, too, is story of introduction of his instruments into France, England, first revelation of their supreme merit, and information on his labels, number of instruments made, prices, mystery of ingredients of his varnish, tone of pre-1684 Stradivari violin and changes between 1684 and 1690. An extremely interesting, informative account for all music lovers, from craftsman to concert-goer. Republication of original (1902) edition. New introduction by Sydney Beck, Head of Rare Book and Manuscript Collections, Music Division, New York Public Library. Analytical index by Rembert Wurlitzer. Appendixes. 68 illustrations. 30 full-page plates. 4 in color. xxvi + 315pp. 5⅜ x 8½.
Paperbound $2.25

Musical Autographs from Monteverdi to Hindemith,
Emanuel Winternitz
For beauty, for intrinsic interest, for perspective on the composer's personality, for subtleties of phrasing, shading, emphasis indicated in the autograph but suppressed in the printed score, the mss. of musical composition are fascinating documents which repay close study in many different ways. This 2-volume work reprints facsimiles of mss. by virtually every major composer, and many minor figures—196 examples in all. A full text points out what can be learned from mss., analyzes each sample. Index. Bibliography. 18 figures. 196 plates. Total of 170pp. of text. 7⅞ x 10¾.
Vol. 1 Paperbound $2.00, Vol. 2 Paperbound $2.00,
The set $4.00

J. S. Bach,
Albert Schweitzer
One of the few great full-length studies of Bach's life and work, and the study upon which Schweitzer's renown as a musicologist rests. On first appearance (1911), revolutionized Bach performance. The only writer on Bach to be musicologist, performing musician, and student of history, theology and philosophy, Schweitzer contributes particularly full sections on history of German Protestant church music, theories on motivic pictorial representations in vocal music, and practical suggestions for performance. Translated by Ernest Newman. Indexes. 5 illustrations. 650 musical examples. Total of xix + 928pp. 5⅜ x 8½.   Vol. 1 Paperbound $2.00, Vol. 2 Paperbound $2.00,
The set $4.00

THE METHODS OF ETHICS, *Henry Sidgwick*

Propounding no organized system of its own, study subjects every major methodological approach to ethics to rigorous, objective analysis. Study discusses and relates ethical thought of Plato, Aristotle, Bentham, Clarke, Butler, Hobbes, Hume, Mill, Spencer, Kant, and dozens of others. Sidgwick retains conclusions from each system which follow from ethical premises, rejecting the faulty. Considered by many in the field to be among the most important treatises on ethical philosophy. Appendix. Index. xlvii + 528pp. 5⅜ x 8½.

Paperbound $2.50

TEUTONIC MYTHOLOGY, *Jakob Grimm*

A milestone in Western culture; the work which established on a modern basis the study of history of religions and comparative religions. 4-volume work assembles and interprets everything available on religious and folkloristic beliefs of Germanic people (including Scandinavians, Anglo-Saxons, etc.). Assembling material from such sources as Tacitus, surviving Old Norse and Icelandic texts, archeological remains, folktales, surviving superstitions, comparative traditions, linguistic analysis, etc. Grimm explores pagan deities, heroes, folklore of nature, religious practices, and every other area of pagan German belief. To this day, the unrivaled, definitive, exhaustive study. Translated by J. S. Stallybrass from 4th (1883) German edition. Indexes. Total of lxxvii + 1887pp. 5⅜ x 8½.   Four volume set, paperbound $10.00

THE I CHING, *translated by James Legge*

Called "The Book of Changes" in English, this is one of the Five Classics edited by Confucius, basic and central to Chinese thought. Explains perhaps the most complex system of divination known, founded on the theory that all things happening at any one time have characteristic features which can be isolated and related. Significant in Oriental studies, in history of religions and philosophy, and also to Jungian psychoanalysis and other areas of modern European thought. Index. Appendixes. 6 plates. xxi + 448pp. 5⅜ x 8½.

Paperbound $2.75

HISTORY OF ANCIENT PHILOSOPHY, *W. Windelband*

One of the clearest, most accurate comprehensive surveys of Greek and Roman philosophy. Discusses ancient philosophy in general, intellectual life in Greece in the 7th and 6th centuries B.C., Thales, Anaximander, Anaximenes, Heraclitus, the Eleatics, Empedocles, Anaxagoras, Leucippus, the Pythagoreans, the Sophists, Socrates, Democritus (20 pages), Plato (50 pages), Aristotle (70 pages), the Peripatetics, Stoics, Epicureans, Sceptics, Neo-platonists, Christian Apologists, etc. 2nd German edition translated by H. E. Cushman. xv + 393pp. 5⅜ x 8.

Paperbound $2.25

THE PALACE OF PLEASURE, *William Painter*

Elizabethan versions of Italian and French novels from *The Decameron*, Cinthio, Straparola, Queen Margaret of Navarre, and other continental sources — the very work that provided Shakespeare and dozens of his contemporaries with many of their plots and sub-plots and, therefore, justly considered one of the most influential books in all English literature. It is also a book that any reader will still enjoy. Total of cviii + 1,224pp.

Three volume set, Paperbound $6.75

THE WONDERFUL WIZARD OF OZ, *L. F. Baum*

All the original W. W. Denslow illustrations in full color—as much a part of "The Wizard" as Tenniel's drawings are of "Alice in Wonderland." "The Wizard" is still America's best-loved fairy tale, in which, as the author expresses it, "The wonderment and joy are retained and the heartaches and nightmares left out." Now today's young readers can enjoy every word and wonderful picture of the original book. New introduction by Martin Gardner. A Baum bibliography. 23 full-page color plates. viii + 268pp. 5⅜ x 8.

Paperbound $1.50

THE MARVELOUS LAND OF OZ, *L. F. Baum*

This is the equally enchanting sequel to the "Wizard," continuing the adventures of the Scarecrow and the Tin Woodman. The hero this time is a little boy named Tip, and all the delightful Oz magic is still present. This is the Oz book with the Animated Saw-Horse, the Woggle-Bug, and Jack Pumpkinhead. All the original John R. Neill illustrations, 10 in full color. 287pp. 5⅜ x 8.

Paperbound $1.50

ALICE'S ADVENTURES UNDER GROUND, *Lewis Carroll*

The original *Alice in Wonderland*, hand-lettered and illustrated by Carroll himself, and originally presented as a Christmas gift to a child-friend. Adults as well as children will enjoy this charming volume, reproduced faithfully in this Dover edition. While the story is essentially the same, there are slight changes, and Carroll's spritely drawings present an intriguing alternative to the famous Tenniel illustrations. One of the most popular books in Dover's catalogue. Introduction by Martin Gardner. 38 illustrations. 128pp. 5⅜ x 8½.

Paperbound $1.00

THE NURSERY "ALICE," *Lewis Carroll*

While most of us consider *Alice in Wonderland* a story for children of all ages, Carroll himself felt it was beyond younger children. He therefore provided this simplified version, illustrated with the famous Tenniel drawings enlarged and colored in delicate tints, for children aged "from Nought to Five." Dover's edition of this now rare classic is a faithful copy of the 1889 printing, including 20 illustrations by Tenniel, and front and back covers reproduced in full color. Introduction by Martin Gardner. xxiii + 67pp. 6⅛ x 9¼.

Paperbound $1.50

THE STORY OF KING ARTHUR AND HIS KNIGHTS, *Howard Pyle*

A fast-paced, exciting retelling of the best known Arthurian legends for young readers by one of America's best story tellers and illustrators. The sword Excalibur, wooing of Guinevere, Merlin and his downfall, adventures of Sir Pellias and Gawaine, and others. The pen and ink illustrations are vividly imagined and wonderfully drawn. 41 illustrations. xviii + 313pp. 6⅛ x 9¼.

Paperbound $1.50

Prices subject to change without notice.

Available at your book dealer or write for free catalogue to Dept. Adsci, Dover Publications, Inc., 180 Varick St., N.Y., N.Y. 10014. Dover publishes more than 150 books each year on science, elementary and advanced mathematics, biology, music, art, literary history, social sciences and other areas.